Elizabeth Gail and Trouble from the Past

Hilda Stahl

Tyndale House Publishers, Inc., Wheaton, Illinois

Dedicated with thanks and love to
my Elizabeth
Elizabeth Dandron

The Elizabeth Gail Series
 1 *Elizabeth Gail and the Mystery at the Johnson Farm*
 2 *Elizabeth Gail and the Secret Box*
 3 *Elizabeth Gail and the Teddy Bear Mystery*
 4 *Elizabeth Gail and the Dangerous Double*
 5 *Elizabeth Gail and the Trouble at the Sandhill Ranch*
 6 *Elizabeth Gail and the Strange Birthday Party*
 7 *Elizabeth Gail and the Terrifying News*
 8 *Elizabeth Gail and the Frightened Runaways*
 9 *Elizabeth Gail and the Trouble from the Past*
10 *Elizabeth Gail and the Silent Piano*
11 *Elizabeth Gail and the Double Trouble*
12 *Elizabeth Gail and the Holiday Mystery*
13 *Elizabeth Gail and the Missing Love Letters*
14 *Elizabeth Gail and the Music Camp Romance*
15 *Elizabeth Gail and the Handsome Stranger*
16 *Elizabeth Gail and the Secret Love*
17 *Elizabeth Gail and the Summer for Weddings*
18 *Elizabeth Gail and the Time for Love*
19 *Elizabeth Gail and the Great Canoe Conspiracy*
20 *Elizabeth Gail and the Hidden Key Mystery*
21 *Elizabeth Gail and the Secret of the Gold Charm*

Copyright © 1981 by Word Spinners, Inc.

Cover and interior illustrations by Kathy Kulin

Library of Congress Catalog Card Number 88-51710
ISBN 0-8423-0804-0

Printed in the United States of America

96 95 94
9   8   7   6   5

Contents

ONE
The new English teacher

Libby looked up as the new English teacher walked into the suddenly quiet room. Oh, she hated to meet a new teacher! It had taken her all of September and October to get used to Miss Morrison. But Miss Morrison had taken a leave of absence to take care of her mother who'd had an operation. Now, Libby would have to meet a new teacher and wait to see if he liked her or hated her. She rubbed her damp palms down her blue denim skirt. A shiver ran down her spine and she thought her heart would jump out of her flowered blouse. She pressed tight against her chair as the man stood behind the large desk in the front of the classroom. He seemed all right. He was short and stocky, but not ugly or mean-looking. Maybe he didn't have anything against aid kids.

She lifted her pointed chin. She was not an aid kid now! Soon she would be adopted by the Johnsons. Then nobody could look down on her and make fun of her! She would belong to a real family who loved her.

The teacher pushed his jacket aside and stood with

his hands resting on his hips. He reminded Libby of Kevin's banty rooster. She had to bite the inside of her lower lip to keep from smiling.

"My name is Mr. Wright, spelled with a *W*," he said in a loud, gruff voice. His gray eyes didn't twinkle and Libby wondered if he was warning everyone not to tease him about being "Right" or "Wrong." Cold November rain lashed against the long windows next to Mr. Wright's desk. "I know that you're used to Miss Morrison and her ways, but now that I'm your teacher, I want things my way without arguments." He walked around the desk and stopped by Susan's desk. He looked down at her but he didn't smile the way most people did when they looked at Susan.

Libby clasped her hands in her lap. If he didn't like Susan Johnson, he sure wouldn't like Libby Dobbs who wasn't a real Johnson yet. When he finally looked at her, her mouth went too dry to swallow.

"We're going to study sentence structure as well as review parts of speech." He leaned back on his desk and folded his arms. "I give a lot of homework and I expect it to be done each night at home and handed in when you walk into class. If you don't, you'll automatically receive a failing grade for that day."

Libby tried to concentrate on all the rules and regulations, but her mind wandered. How long would it be before she was Elizabeth Gail Johnson instead of Elizabeth Gail Dobbs? Susan, Ben, and Kevin were born into the Johnson family. Toby was nine and he was already adopted. He thought he was so big! *She* wouldn't act like such a hot shot when she got adopted!

A hand gripped her shoulder and she almost jumped out of her seat. She looked up into Mr. Wright's stern face. She wanted to slide out of sight under her desk.

"I said to open your book to page fifteen. One-five. Fifteen. And after you find it I want you to go to the board and diagram the first sentence."

She fumbled with her book as he walked away. The book plopped to the floor and the girl behind her giggled and jabbed her with the end of her pencil. As Libby picked up the book she looked up at the boy beside her. The book fell from her tense fingers again and several people laughed.

Could that boy really be Jerry Grosbeck? His hair was longer than it had been, but from the side of his right eye to his jaw was the same white, puckered scar. His eyes narrowed as he stared at her, then he looked straight ahead. Why hadn't she noticed that there was a new boy in class? And Jerry Grosbeck at that!

"Libby Dobbs, get to the board," snapped Mr. Wright.

With her book clutched tight against her, Libby walked to the front of the room. What had he told her to do? Her face burned as she realized everyone's eyes were on her. She felt tall and skinny and ugly. That morning Libby had used the curling iron on her hair but now it hung limp and straggly. Maybe Jerry Grosbeck hadn't recognized her since she didn't have braids, baggy, unkempt clothes, and a dirty face.

Libby picked up a piece of white chalk and looked down at her book. The words blurred before her eyes.

What had Mr. Wright asked her to do? Her stomach cramped and she thought she was going to be sick.

"What are you waiting for?" asked Mr. Wright.

Libby wanted to sink through the floor. She stared down at her tan shoes and noticed that one lace had come untied.

"Who will volunteer to diagram that sentence?" Mr. Wright paused and Libby kept her head down, her back to the class. "Joanne Tripper, you may take Libby's place at the board."

Libby crept back to her seat and sank down. Naturally it was Joanne Tripper!

"Libby, you must write one hundred times, 'I will listen in class at all times,'" said Mr. Wright sharply. "Hand it in with your homework tomorrow."

Libby gripped her book tighter and wanted to tell Mr. Wright what he could do with his sentences and his homework, but she couldn't. Once she would have, but now that she was a Christian, she couldn't. Chuck had told her often that it was important to be like Jesus. And Jesus wouldn't talk back to Mr. Wright.

Susan looked back and smiled and it made Libby feel a little better. But then she looked over at Jerry Grosbeck and he was laughing at her under his breath the way she remembered that he had and she wanted to punch him. She forced herself to watch Joanne diagram the sentence. Libby could tell that Joanne loved all the attention she was getting. She flipped her blonde hair and her skirt swung around her slender legs as she turned and walked back to her seat. She smiled triumphantly down at Libby, then went on to her seat behind her. Libby waited,

10

then sure enough, a pencil jabbed her in the back. She pretended not to notice as Mr. Wright kept on talking, but Joanne poked her again. She looked over her shoulder and Joanne looked haughtily at her.

"I can do everything better than you," she whispered.

Libby shrugged and turned back. One of these days she'd break every one of Joanne's pencils.

Finally the bell rang and Libby jumped up amidst the noises of loud voices and the scraping of moving chairs. She started toward the door, then stopped. Jerry Grosbeck stood beside the door, watching her, waiting for her. She wanted to turn and jump out a window or go into the small book room just behind Mr. Wright's desk and pretend she had to get a book.

"Let's go to lunch, Libby," said Susan, tugging on her arm.

Libby hesitated, then walked reluctantly toward the door and Jerry Grosbeck.

TWO
Jerry Grosbeck

"What's wrong with you, Libby?" Susan nudged Libby impatiently. "Hurry up. I'm hungry."

Libby wanted to turn the other way, but she walked a little faster toward the door and Jerry Grosbeck. Why didn't he leave? What would he say to her after two years? The loud shouts and laughter of the students made her head throb. She pretended that he wasn't standing beside the door watching her. She pretended that he didn't exist but she felt stiff and awkward and she was afraid he'd notice.

She jumped when he touched her arm. Her face flushed red as she looked at him.

"Hi, Libby. I want to talk to you."

She licked her dry lips. "I'm going to lunch with Susan."

"I want to talk."

She cleared her throat as she turned to Susan. "I'll meet you in the lunchroom in a few minutes." She saw the look Susan gave Jerry before she hurried down the crowded hall. She knew Susan's curiosity was going wild.

"You look different, Libby."

She looked at Jerry, then quickly down at the floor. He looked the same. His clothes didn't fit his thin body and he smelled the same—as if he hadn't taken a bath for a month. His brown hair was oily and tangled, but hung to his collar and almost in his eyes. When they'd lived with the Adairs, Mrs. Adair had always kept his unruly brown hair cropped off almost to his scalp.

"Where do you live now?" Jerry sounded impatient and angry. "You hit a gold mine or something?"

She caught her breath. They had talked about what they would do if they ever got rich and didn't have to be ragged and dirty and live off the state. "I'm going to be adopted by a nice family."

"That's a laugh. Who would want Libby Dobbs, meanest girl in the world?"

Her head jerked up and her hazel eyes flashed. "Who says I am?"

He laughed under his breath and shook his head. "I say. I should know. You beat me up enough times."

"And you deserved it every time!" She doubled her fists at her sides and felt she was ten years old again instead of twelve. "You were always telling on me so I'd get beaten. And you'd take my food and I'd have to go hungry because Mrs. Adair wouldn't believe me."

"You're still skinny even if you do have nice clothes that fit you."

"I'm going to lunch." She turned away but he caught her arm and his grip hurt. She looked back at him with a scowl. "Let me go!"

"Remember that bronze medal of my dad's that you took from me?" His brown eyes were dark with emotion and for a minute she felt sorry for him.

"I remember."

"I want it back."

She swallowed hard. "I thought I gave it back to you."

He dropped his arm and shook his head. "You were going to but Miss Miller took me away to another home and you were gone and I couldn't find it in your room."

She had known how important that medal was to him but she'd wanted to do the worst thing to him that she could think of. "I'll see if I have it in my stuff at home. I'll give it back if I find it."

"See that you do! Oh, I hated you for taking that from me! It was the only thing I had of Dad's; now I don't have anything." He looked down but not before she saw tears sparkling in his eyes.

"I'm sorry I took it, Jerry."

He looked up in surprise. "I didn't know you knew that word, Libby. You are different."

"Libby!"

She turned, then smiled as April and May Brakie walked up to her. They gasped in surprise when they saw Jerry.

"When did you start school here?" asked April, her brown eyes wide. "I heard you were in a detention home."

"You heard wrong." Jerry's face flushed and he pushed past the girls and hurried down the almost empty hall toward the lunchroom.

"What a surprise," said May, shaking her head as she looked after Jerry.

"He's in my English class," said Libby as she

sagged against the wall. "He started today. I couldn't believe it."

"We're going to lunch, Libby. Want to come with us?" April smiled questioningly. She was dressed in a blue sweater and blue cords identical to her twin's, but Libby could tell them apart in her own special way. She'd learned to when they'd lived in a foster home together.

Libby nodded and walked with them down the hall. They asked her about Jerry, but she didn't have much to tell them. She hadn't asked him who he was living with. She hadn't asked him if he was happy. Tears filled her eyes. She already knew the answer to that. He was as unhappy today as he had been when they'd lived with the Adairs. Did he still run away regularly? Who was his caseworker now that Miss Miller was married to Uncle Luke?

May tugged Libby's short brown hair. "Forget about Jerry Grosbeck. He can take care of himself. He always has."

"Did you know he had a chance to be adopted once?" asked April, lifting her eyebrows.

Libby stopped in surprise. "And he didn't get adopted?"

"Nope. He said he'd only live with his real dad. He said that his dad would come for him someday and he couldn't be tied down to a family. He ran away from them and Miss Miller put him in with that terrible Mrs. Smith. Remember her?"

May nodded and made a face. "I wouldn't want a dog to live with her!"

"I never had to live with her. Miss Miller found out what she was like and had her license taken away."

Libby walked toward the lunchroom, her skirt swinging around her thin legs. "Susan will be waiting for us."

Susan had saved a place at a table for the girls and they filled their trays and hurried to her. Libby could see that Susan was ready to burst.

"What did he want? Who was he?" Susan bounced on her chair and her red-gold hair flipped around as if it were alive. Her blue eyes sparkled and Libby knew she wouldn't quit asking until she knew everything.

"His name is Jerry Grosbeck," said May as she pushed her fork into the pile of ravioli.

"He's an aid kid," said April.

"But what did he want with you, Libby?"

Libby swallowed a drink of chocolate milk. "I took something of his when we lived at the same foster home. He wants it back."

"It's his medal, I bet," said April, leaning forward excitedly. "He thinks if he has it, his dad will come back and get him to live with him."

"That will never happen," said Libby impatiently. She looked up and Jerry Grosbeck stood beside the table, his face almost as white as the scar running down the side of his face. She covered her mouth with her trembling hand. Why hadn't she kept her big mouth shut?

"It will happen!" shouted Jerry, shoving hard against Libby and knocking her from her seat. "You're nothing but a stupid aid kid! You don't know anything!"

Libby felt on fire with embarrassment as she stood up. She hated to have everyone staring at her.

"Go away, Jerry," said April in a low, stern voice. "You'll make trouble for all of us. Get away from here."

Libby saw the lunchroom supervisor looking in their direction. "Go on, Jerry. I'll get your medal for you if I still have it. I might have tossed it out or something." She knew the minute the words were out that she shouldn't have said them.

He grabbed her by the arms and shook her hard. "You stole my medal! You ruined my life!"

Before the supervisor could reach them, Jerry ran from the lunchroom, his dirty tennis shoes slapping on the floor in the sudden silence.

"You girls all right?" asked the supervisor as she walked up to them with a frown. "We don't want trouble in here."

"We're just fine," said Susan with one of her best smiles.

"Just keep down the noise in the future." The supervisor frowned toward the door, then walked back toward the line of food.

"Let's get out of here," whispered Libby as she picked up her tray. She couldn't stand the attention she was getting. She wanted to crawl into a hole out of sight or hide in the restroom.

"It wasn't your fault," said May. "His dad won't come back for him. His dad's probably dead."

"Don't talk about it," snapped Libby. She walked away, her head high and her back very stiff.

"Making trouble wherever you go," said Joanne Tripper, stepping in front of Libby. "That's one thing you're better at than I am."

"Leave her alone," said Susan firmly. "This is none of your business, Joanne."

Libby walked around Joanne and set her tray in place, then rushed from the lunchroom. The last time she'd been this embarrassed in the lunchroom was when Brenda Wilkens had picked a fight with her. Since she'd made friends with Brenda, she thought she had no more enemies. Now, Joanne Tripper and Jerry Grosbeck were against her.

"Wait, Libby." Susan caught her arm. "I have to go to the library. Come with me."

"No! I want to be alone. Take the twins and go." Libby pulled free and rushed down the nearly empty hall toward the restroom.

THREE
Joanne Tripper

Libby leaned weakly against the sink in the girls'
restroom. Would she ever be without enemies? Would
she ever learn to stay out of trouble? She looked up
and saw wide hazel eyes staring back at her. Her face
was still red. With trembling hands she splashed cold
water on her hot face. She patted it dry and tossed
the paper towel into the large wastebasket. She
turned as the door burst open. Joanne Tripper stood
in the doorway.

"I've been looking for you, Libby."

"You found me." Libby turned away tiredly.

Joanne stepped into the room and the door
swooshed shut behind her. She flipped her long
blonde hair over her shoulder. "I'm going to ask you
one more time, Libby."

Libby sighed. "The answer is still no. I don't see
why you should think I'd be willing to give up piano
lessons with Rachel Avery just so you could take from
her."

Joanne knotted her fists at her sides. "You stupid

aid kid! Momma says I *have* to take from Rachael Avery. Momma says that an aid kid doesn't deserve to take lessons from a famous concert pianist."

"You tell Momma that I *am* taking lessons. I am going to be a famous concert pianist. I won't give up my dream for anyone! I mean it, Joanne."

Joanne shook her head with an impatient sigh. She stood with her hands on her narrow waist and the soft material of her burnt orange dress showed off her figure just the way she wanted it to. Libby knew that Joanne always dressed to impress others, mostly the teachers, but some of the more important students also. "Look at you, Libby. You don't look like a concert pianist. I do! You look more like the aid kid you are."

Libby locked her hands together behind her back. She would not punch Joanne in the nose. "I won't quit lessons." Why wouldn't Joanne leave her alone? For almost three weeks now she'd been pestering her about it.

"Momma says you will." Joanne's eyes narrowed as she stepped closer to Libby. "Momma says I'm the one who should be taking from Rachael Avery. And I'm going to! I'll do whatever I have to to make you stop."

"Nothing will make me stop!" Libby's heart raced as she tried to think what Joanne could do to carry out her threat.

Joanne looked down her pretty nose at Libby. "Momma knows your real mother. Momma says she'll tell Rachael Avery all about Marie Dobbs, then Rachael won't want you." Joanne turned and pulled open the door and walked out.

Libby's heart raced and a bitter taste filled her

mouth. How could Joanne's mother be so mean? How could Joanne?

Libby jerked open the door and looked wildly up and down the hall for Joanne. She saw her disappear into the science room. Libby rushed down the hall and into the room. Joanne stood at the project table. She turned and looked up at Libby. The smells in the room made Libby's stomach churn.

"Joanne, Rachael already knows about Mother. Your momma can't tell her anything to make her stop my lessons."

Joanne smiled and lifted her brows. "Oh? You just wait, Libby."

Libby pressed her thin lips together tightly. She would never give up her dream! Someday she would be Elizabeth Gail Johnson, concert pianist! Nothing, no one, could stop her! "I won't fight with you, Joanne." Libby turned to leave but Joanne grabbed her arms and jerked her back. Joanne's long, strong fingers bit into Libby's thin arm.

"I'm not finished with you, aid kid!"

"Let me go," Libby said through her teeth.

"Make me, aid kid!"

"Don't call me that!"

"Aid kid!"

With her free hand Libby grabbed a handful of Joanne's bright hair and pulled. Joanne screamed and slapped Libby's face with a blow that stung.

"Girls!"

Libby jerked her head around to find Mr. Wright standing in the doorway, his hands on his hips. The room seemed to spin as he walked toward them.

"What's going on here?"

"She started it," said Joanne, pointing at Libby. "I came in here to work on my project and she followed me in and started a fight."

Libby tried to speak but her voice was locked in her throat. She stared at Mr. Wright and knew that he would believe Joanne instead of her anyway. Teachers never believed aid kids, even ones that were going to be adopted.

Mr. Wright shook his head. "You like bringing trouble on yourself, don't you? Would you like me to report you or call your parents?"

Libby shook her head. It was hard to breathe and she was afraid she would faint.

"I told her not to fight in school," said Joanne with tears in her big blue eyes. "I told her, but she wouldn't listen."

"I won't report this today, but if either of you causes any more trouble or if you fight again, you'll both end up in the principal's office. Now, get to your next class. It's almost time for the bell."

Libby walked from the room on shaky legs. Two times in one day she'd gotten into trouble with the new teacher! Not even she should have that happen!

Joanne jabbed Libby with the eraser of her pencil. "I'm not beat yet. You'll see!"

Libby glared at her. "I hope you never get to take lessons from Rachael Avery! I hope your fingers curl up into short little stubs that hurt when you even touch the piano!"

Joanne gasped, her hand at her mouth, her eyes wide. "Don't say that!"

"If Rachael ever has room for you, I hope she says

you're too poor a player for her to bother with!"

"Stop it! Stop it! Momma won't let that happen!"
Joanne rushed away with tears streaming down her
pale cheeks.

Libby tossed her head and walked to her locker and
pulled out her history book. Joanne deserved to be
scared. Libby turned and bumped into Jerry
Grosbeck.

He frowned angrily. "I won't forget what you said
about Dad, Libby."

Libby's anger bubbled up and over. "I hope I never
find that medal. And if I do, I'll throw it away and
you'll never get it back!"

Jerry pushed his face close to hers and she could
smell his bad breath. "I hope you never get adopted! I
hope this family finds out what a rotten girl you are
and kicks you out!"

Libby shivered and pulled back. It would be
terrible if they knew just how bad she really was.
What would Chuck and Vera do if they learned that
she'd been fighting in school? What would they do if
they knew she'd said hateful things to Joanne and
Jerry?

Before she could say anything more, Susan walked
up and told her they had to get to history class right
now or they'd be tardy. She peeked back, then looked
quickly ahead as they walked. Jerry was right behind
them. He was going to be in history also. She would
not do or say anything to get in more trouble during
the next hour.

The bell rang just as Libby sank down in her seat.
Thankfully, Jerry sat across the room from her. She

wouldn't have to smell him or see him. She'd pay attention in class and forget about both Jerry and Joanne Tripper.

"I see we have a new boy in class," said Mr. Coons after he'd taken roll.

From the corner of her eye Libby saw Joanne's hand shoot up.

"Yes, Joanne." Mr. Coons adjusted his glasses and cleared his throat.

"The new boy is a friend of Libby's. Why don't you put him beside her?"

Labby sank low in her seat as her cheeks flushed red. Joanne was going to get it good!

"I'm glad Jerry has a friend in school already. Jerry, you may sit just ahead of Libby."

Libby kept her eyes on the carved initials in the desk. She heard Jerry sit in front of her. She smelled him, too.

"Welcome to class and to this school, Jerry," said Mr. Coons with his bright smile. "If you need any help, call on me."

Libby heard Joanne snicker, then cough to cover it up. Oh, Joanne was really asking for it!

"Open your books to page fifty-three, class."

Libby opened her book and tried to listen to Mr. Coons. Jerry dropped a paper on the floor and kicked it back to Libby. She looked down, then flushed at the bad word on the paper. She hadn't used that word since she'd become a Christian. She looked up and Mr. Coons was looking right at her. Had he asked her a question?

"What is the problem, Libby?" he asked as he walked toward her.

She coughed. "Nothing." Frantically she tried to cover the word with her foot but Mr. Coons spotted the paper and bent to pick it up.

"Libby! I'm surprised at you." He crumpled the paper and tossed it into the wastebasket. "I know you have better ways to occupy your time."

Libby swallowed hard and wanted to hide from everyone, especially Mr. Coons. She knew he was a Christian and that he was a friend of Chuck. What if he told Chuck about the word on the paper? Would Chuck believe her if she said she hadn't written it?

She saw Jerry's shoulders shake with silent laughter and she wanted to hit him in the back. She would have jabbed him with her pencil but she was afraid he'd tell on her and she'd be in more trouble. Already this day had been filled with trouble for her. What had she done to cause it?

She leaned back in her chair and tried to keep the tears from showing in her eyes. It would be too embarrassing to cry in front of everyone, especially Joanne Tripper. Joanne would love to make her cry.

Libby blinked hard and sat very still. She would not cry! She would listen to Mr. Coons. Just what should she do to get even with Joanne and Jerry? She sure would think of something terrible!

FOUR
Homework

Libby pushed the barn door closed against the cold rain and rushed down the aisle to Snowball's stall. Snowball nickered a happy greeting. Libby pressed her face against the white filly's neck. "I had such a terrible day today, Snowball. I wish I could have stayed right here with you and not gone to school at all!" The humiliation swept over her again and the tears filled her eyes. "I don't want to go to school again. I don't want to see the teachers or the kids. And I never want to see that terrible Joanne Tripper or that gross Jerry Grosbeck again." Just thinking of gross Jerry Grosbeck made her giggle.

"Gross Jerry Grosbeck," she said and laughed until Snowball blew against her arm. "Don't you think it's funny, Snowball?"

Libby fed the horses, feeling much better. Maybe she wouldn't try to get even with Joanne and Jerry. Maybe she'd just forget the whole miserable day.

A barn cat rubbed against her leg and she picked it up and held it close, listening to the loud purr. She remembered just two months ago when she'd found April and May hidden in the barn beside the bales of hay. They had run away from bad foster parents and come to Libby for help. She smiled. Chuck had helped find the twins a home with a Christian family. Now, the girls were happy living with Chris and Jean Allison.

Libby smiled as she remembered how they'd all agreed together in prayer for the right family for the twins. The Lord had answered! And he had answered a long time ago when the Johnsons had prayed her into their family. She pressed the cat closer to her. She was loved after all the years of being hated and kicked around and living from foster home to foster home. Part of the time she'd lived with Mother, but Mother had always deserted her and Miss Miller would come for her and find her another foster home.

"But not any more! I'm going to be adopted!" Libby twirled around the barn, then set the cat on the bales of hay. Mother had signed the paper saying that she could be adopted. "You hear that, kitty? Maybe by the time I'm thirteen years old, I'll belong to this family for real." The cat purred louder and Libby laughed again. "You're happy for me, aren't you?"

A few minutes later Libby ran through the cold rain to the back porch. She pulled off her wet coat and hung it on a hook beside Susan's old blue barn coat. They all worked together on outdoor as well as indoor chores. Libby liked taking care of the horses and calves the best. She was glad that Kevin and Toby did the chicken chores. She didn't like the chickens or Goosy Poosy as well as she liked the other animals on the large farm. Ben had showed her how to hook up the milkers on the cows, but she didn't like doing it. She liked feeding the calves and doctoring sick or injured animals.

The smell of roast beef drifted onto the back porch and Libby's stomach growled. She couldn't wait for Chuck to come home from his store in town so they could eat. She turned around and almost bumped into Kevin. He blinked hard behind his glasses and pushed his soft blond hair away from his forehead.

"Mom says we can play a game of Clue before supper, Elizabeth."

She smiled. She liked to have people call her Elizabeth. Someday she wouldn't use her nickname at all. Everyone would call her Elizabeth and she'd even think of herself as Elizabeth instead of Libby. Libby was not the name for a concert pianist!

"I have homework to do first, Kevin, then I'll play Clue if I have time." She didn't like to play Clue as well as Monopoly. It was hard to think and remember enough to know what cards were hidden in the small black envelope. Monopoly was fun with all the money and property. Kevin liked Clue better because he wanted to be a detective when he grew up. He liked to solve crimes and mysteries.

"Work fast, Elizabeth." Kevin walked beside Libby to the family room. A fire crackled in the large fireplace at the end of the room. Libby wanted to rush to the piano along the wall and play and play instead of doing her homework.

"I'll help you, Elizabeth," said Kevin, looking up at her. His head just reached to her shoulder.

She wished she could have him write the sentences for the new English teacher, but she didn't dare tell him about that. "No thanks, Kevin. I'll get done as soon as I can." She picked up her books from the small table near the door and sat cross-legged on the carpet in front of the warm, crackling fire.

She wrote the sentences first. Her hand ached from holding the pencil tightly. She wrinkled her nose at the two pages of work she still had to do. It wasn't fair for Mr. Wright to give them so much homework. How could she do all her chores, practice the piano, and do homework before bedtime?

Just as she finished Ben rushed into the room. "Quick! The calves are out! Help me get them back in!"

Libby jumped to her feet and rushed to get her jacket with Toby and Kevin and Ben with her. Susan joined them and they rushed outdoors. The rain had stopped and cold wind cut against Libby's face and she shivered. She ran along the driveway to head off a black and white calf. She stepped into a puddle and felt cold water soak into her sock. It would take her boot a long time to dry.

"Get that one, Toby!" she shouted, pointing toward the horse barn. She watched Toby run fast and turn the calf toward the cow barn and the pen beside it where the calves were kept. Toby's red hair flopped up and down as he ran. His freckles stood out on his face and his jacket hung open and flapped wildly.

Finally Ben closed and locked the gate on the last calf. He laughed, his hazel eyes sparkling. He pushed his red hair back. "We make good cowboys, don't we? All we need are ropes and cow ponies." He suddenly turned to Libby. "That reminds me, Elizabeth. You got a letter today from your cowboy from Nebraska, Mark McCall." Ben laughed and Libby did, too.

"Where is it?" She remembered the fun they'd had when they'd visited the Nebraska ranch and seen what her real dad had left to her when he'd died.

"Did I get one?" asked Susan, jumping up and down. "Did I?"

"If you did, it's inside the envelope with Libby's," said Ben. "Here it is." He pulled the crumpled envelope out of his pocket and handed it to Libby. "I meant to give it to you when you were feeding the calves a while ago, but I forgot. Sorry."

"That's all right, Ben." Libby ripped open the envelope and pulled out a single page. "There isn't a letter for you, Susan."

"Let me read yours, Libby. Please, oh, please!"

Libby frowned. "No! It's my letter, Susan."

Susan's shoulders slumped and her mouth drooped and Libby felt sorry. "All right, Susan. You can read it after I finish."

Susan hugged Libby, then let her go. "Quick! Read it! Read it!"

Libby walked slowly toward the house, reading as she walked. Mark said that he liked school, but he liked better working with the horses on the ranch. He said he and Old Zeb were good friends and that Old Zeb had been going to church with them often. Mark said even Nolen Brown was his friend. Libby looked up and smiled. "Susan, he says he'll write to you later."

"I hope we get to go to Nebraska again in the summer," said Toby wistfully. "I want to go again."

"Sure, and see Vickie McCall and have her chase you around again," said Kevin, punching Toby's arm playfully. "You wanted her to kiss you."

"I did not!" Toby's face flushed a bright red. "You wanted her to kiss you!"

Libby laughed as she walked into the house with the others close behind. She watched Susan read Mark's letter, then reread it. Susan really liked Mark McCall. Libby wanted to grab the letter away and tell Susan never to touch her mail again. But she didn't. She took the letter when Susan held it out to her and she folded it back into the envelope. She'd put it in her desk later and read it at bedtime when she was alone. Tonight, she'd answer it. Maybe she'd tell Mark about her terrible day. But maybe she'd only tell him about chasing the calves back in the pen.

"Kids, come to supper," said Vera, standing in the doorway as they pulled off the jackets. "Dad called and said to eat without him. He'll be late."

Libby smiled at Vera and felt proud that soon she'd really be her mother. Libby liked Vera's blonde shoulder-length hair and her pretty blue eyes. The red checked skirt and blouse looked nice on her.

Libby's stomach growled as she sat at the large dining room table. She didn't like the empty chair at the head of the table where Chuck should have been. Once in a while he had to miss supper with them. Libby liked to see him at the table, talking and laughing with all of them, listening to how the day went for everyone. After supper he would read from the Bible and they would pray together. Often Vera

would read a book to them. The day was not the same with Chuck gone.

He came home just as Libby and Susan finished the dishes. Libby heard Chuck laughing as he walked toward the kitchen. She rushed to him and threw her arms around him. His red hair was tousled from the wind. "I am so glad to see you, Dad!"

"I missed you, Elizabeth." He kissed her and she thought her heart would burst with happiness. She kept hold of his arm as he hugged and kissed Susan. Susan was little and dainty and Libby felt tall and awkward.

"I'm hungry," he said, looking around the kitchen. "What did you leave me for supper?"

Vera laughed and said, "Almost nothing," but she took his dinner out of the oven and he sat at the table and ate. Libby and Susan sat with him and talked to him. Susan told about the letter from Mark, and Libby wanted to punch her for telling him before she could.

Just then Kevin walked in. "Libby, come play Clue with Ben and me."

Libby hesitated, then agreed since Vera was talking with Chuck about her day. Kevin tried to tell her how to mark her paper so that she had a better chance to win the game, but she couldn't understand what he meant. She sat on the chair across from Ben at the game table, then looked around the room. She had forgotten to take care of her homework and her school book. Finally she saw it lying on the hearth. She walked over and picked up her book and looked inside for the papers. They weren't inside. She looked around the room, but didn't see them. "Where's my homework?"

"Homework?" asked Kevin with a puzzled frown.

"I had several papers with this book on the floor."

Kevin slapped his hand over his mouth and his eyes were wide behind his glasses. "I thought those were old papers and I burned them in the fireplace."

"You what?" screamed Libby, grabbing his arms. "You what?"

"I'm really sorry, Elizabeth. Honest. I didn't know. I'm sorry." He looked ready to burst into tears and that made Libby angrier still.

"You should be sorry! You should do the homework for me now!"

"What's all this yelling?" asked Chuck sharply as he walked into the family room. "Elizabeth, what is wrong with you?"

She turned to him, her thin chest rising and falling. She tried to speak and couldn't. She heard Ben explain what had happened, then she burst into tears and Chuck pulled her close.

"Honey, we're all very sorry that it happened. But it did happen and you'll have to redo your homework. I'm very sorry."

She pulled away from Chuck and glared at Kevin. She'd never forgive him for what he'd done. The rest of her day was ruined. Now she wouldn't have time to practice her piano. She turned and stalked out of the room and up the stairs to her room. She'd find a way to get even with Kevin!

FIVE
Serious thinking

Libby dropped her finished homework on Mr. Wright's desk and tried to forget the talk Chuck had had with her before she went to sleep last night. She did not want to think about forgiving Kevin for burning her homework! He didn't deserve to be forgiven. She wouldn't think about what the Bible said about it. Maybe after she stopped being angry at Kevin, she could forgive him.

"What's wrong with you, aid kid?" asked Joanne, jabbing Libby with her pencil. "Did you get kicked out of the Johnsons' house?"

Libby turned with an angry frown. "Shut up!" She turned back around and clutched her book until her knuckles turned white. Would they kick her out if she didn't forgive Kevin?

Something stung against her arm and she jerked. Something stung the side of her face and she saw a small paper wad land on the floor next to her foot. She looked across in time to see Jerry Grosbeck aiming another paper wad at her, the rubber band stretched long. She frowned at him and he released the rubber band and the missile flew toward her. She moved and it struck her on the shoulder. Before she could say anything Mr. Wright walked into the room and started taking roll. She glared at Jerry and his shoulders moved with silent laughter. She faced forward and refused to glance at him the rest of the class period. When the bell rang she hurried toward the door, knowing Susan was close behind. Just as she walked past Jerry she tripped, stumbled, and plopped to the floor. She looked quickly around to see who had noticed, her face brick red. Awkwardly she pushed herself up without too many people noticing her fall. She could tell by Jerry's face that he had tripped her on purpose. Susan caught her arm and urged her toward the door.

"Don't yell at him," whispered Susan. "Mr. Wright was watching you to see what you would do. You don't want him to think you're a troublemaker, do you?"

Libby rubbed her elbow where it had struck the corner of a desk as she fell. She took a deep breath and tried to hide her anger. She didn't want Susan to know that she felt like beating Jerry up until he couldn't move. Susan would tell the family, and Libby didn't want Chuck and Vera to know.

But God knew *everything* about her life and her thoughts and her actions.

The thought made her feel strange. Why did she always forget that God knew her? He was always with her and he cared for her.

"What's the matter, Libby?" asked Susan with a frown.

"I . . . I was just thinking." Libby walked slowly toward the lunchroom. She sure wasn't being like Jesus the way she'd promised him that she'd be. She was being the old Libby, the Libby that Jerry had known.

She stood in line in the lunchroom with the sounds of clattering silverware, clinking plates and shouts and laughter and thought about the day several months ago that she'd accepted Jesus as her personal Savior. She had first thought that the Johnsons were strange, then realized that being Christians, being Christ-like, was a way of life to them. They taught her love, then finally she'd accepted God's love. Was she any different now than she had been then? Chuck had said that a person grows from a baby Christian into a mature one. Had she grown at all?

Automatically Libby filled her tray and walked to a table with Susan. Had seeing Jerry again made her forget the new Libby, the recreated Libby? Chuck had told her that once she accepted Christ, he made her a new creature, that her old life was dead and she was alive in Christ. Had Jerry brought back the old life? Was that possible?

"The ckicken is good today, Libby," said Susan, rubbing her fingers on a white paper napkin. If you don't want yours, I'll eat it."

Libby looked at her plate absently, then picked up the chicken leg and laid it on Susan's plate. Libby didn't feel hungry at all. She felt terrible for the way she had treated Kevin. And she really should find Jerry and tell him that she would look tonight for his medal and give it to him if she found it. She looked around the lunchroom. Jerry was just walking out the door. She pushed back her chair. "Susan, I'll see you in class later. I have to talk to Jerry right now."

"Don't fight with him," Susan said with her mouth full of food.

"I won't." Libby pushed her hair back nervously. "Will you take care of my tray, please?"

"Sure, Libby. I'll eat your food first."

Libby hurried toward the door. She had to find Jerry before she lost her nerve. The hall was almost empty. Two boys stood beside the water fountain and a girl leaned against her locker. Jerry was not in sight. Maybe it would be better to look for the medal tonight and give it to him Monday in school and not say anything to him now. She rubbed her hands down her dark brown cords and shook her head. She'd better find him and tell him. She had to let him now that she was sorry for being mean to him. He had to know that she wasn't the old Libby Dobbs, but the new Libby who was trying to be the image of Christ.

She walked around a corner, then stopped, her heart racing. Jerry was standing close to the boy in school who peddled drugs. Would Jerry get into drugs? Maybe he already had. She took a deep breath and walked fast down the hall, her eyes glued to Jerry. He had to look up and see her before he did something he would be sorry for.

She stopped beside him and he jumped guiltily. "Can I talk to you, Jerry?" Her voice sounded high and squeaky."

"I'm busy right now." Jerry turned to Ralph Bauer and Libby wanted to turn and run back to Susan.

"Jerry, it's important." Libby's face felt hot and she could barely talk around the tightness of her throat.

42

"Better talk to her, Grosbeck, then we can get back to our business." Ralph Bauer shoved his hands into his pockets and hunched his thin shoulders. "I'll meet you in the restroom later." He walked away, whistling off-key.

"This better be good, Libby! I've got business with Bauer."

"Stop acting like a tough eighth-grader." Libby shook her head with a frown. "Don't get into drugs, Jerry. It's not good for you."

"What do you care?" He pushed his unruly hair away from his face but it flopped back down. His nose looked too big for his face. "Say what you wanted to say to me and let me out of here."

"You're not making this easy." She locked her fingers together and twisted her toe. "I'm going to look for your medal tonight and I'll give it to you Monday if I find it. I'm sorry for being mean to you." She saw the surprise on his face and she smiled. "I mean it, Jerry."

Jerry laughed. "It's a joke. Right?"

"No."

"When do you punch me in the nose?"

"I won't at all."

He scratched his head. "I don't get it."

"I told you I'm different." Libby fumbled with the *E* hanging on the gold chain around her neck. "I'm a Christian now."

"And you go to church?"

She nodded.

"And pray?"

"Yes."

He shook his head. "You're faking, aren't you?

You'll do anything to get adopted and you're doing this so your new family will adopt you."

"I am not!"

"I stayed with a Christian family about two months. They beat me every day and more on Sunday. Mrs. Blevins got me out of there and told me never to trust a Christian."

"I know a lot of Christians, Jerry. I don't know any that are bad. Dad says that some people think they're

Christians but if they don't trust Jesus and try to be like him, then they're fooling themselves. Maybe the people you knew weren't really born-again Christians."

Jerry pushed his hands into his baggy gray pants. "I don't want to waste time talking about all this dumb stuff. You make sure you get me my medal and we'll be even."

"Don't get mixed up with Bauer—please, Jerry!"

Jerry frowned. "Why should you care? Are you my mother or something? You sure don't look like one."

Several boys walked toward them and Libby told Jerry she'd talk to him again Monday. She hurried away from him and turned the corner to find Joanne Tripper waiting for her.

"You and that new boy sure have a lot to talk about, don't you? I bet you like having another aid kid around." Joanne flipped her blonde hair back. "I watched you talking to Ralph Bauer. I'm going to tell Mr. Page you were buying drugs."

"Don't you dare! That's a lie and you know it!" Libby doubled her fists at her sides. How could Joanne be so mean?

"Momma says you aid kids are always freaking out on drugs. She says you won't always want to play the piano and take lessons from Rachael Avery. Momma says she'll make sure I get in with Rachael."

Libby stamped her foot. "Leave me alone, Joanne Tripper! You can't make trouble for me!"

"I won't if you'll talk to Rachael Avery in the morning when you go in for a lesson and tell her you're quitting. Momma says Rachael will take me as soon as she has room for me."

Libby walked away as quickly as she could. How could she stop Joanne from harassing her all the time? One of these days Joanne just might find herself sitting on the floor with a very bloody nose and if "Momma" was anywhere around, she would be right beside her precious daughter!

And what kind of Christian would she be if she did that? She had to find a way to stop Joanne. Was it too hard even for the Lord?

SIX
Rachael Avery

Libby sat at the baby grand piano in Rachael Avery's music room. The warm sunlight streamed through the window onto the music that Libby was going to play today. Lovingly, she touched the keys. She knew she was going to play well today. She'd had to miss only one night of practice.

"You look very pleased with yourself, Elizabeth." Rachael sat on the stool beside the piano bench. Two pink barrettes that matched her pink blouse held her long black hair away from her face. "Let's see what you've accomplished this week."

Libby smiled with assurance as she touched the keys. Inside her head she didn't hear the simple songs she played, but she heard her fingers running up and down the keyboard, playing the way Rachael had played in concert. Libby's heart raced excitedly. Someday the songs coming from her fingertips would match the songs inside her head and her heart. People would stand up and clap and cheer because of her music. Rachael Avery would proudly announce that she had trained the well-known Elizabeth Johnson. And Rachael would say that even at her best she wasn't as good as Elizabeth.

"That was very good, Elizabeth." Rachael smiled and Libby could hear the thunderous applause. "I'll show you what to practice for next Saturday." She paused and Libby saw a strange expression on her face. "Unless you won't be back."

Did Rachael mean she didn't want her back? Libby's stomach tightened. "I'll be here!"

"Please give me notice if you won't be."

Libby tried to move, but couldn't. "What do you mean?" Was that hoarse voice coming from her?

"I understand that you'll be quitting."

Libby gasped, her eyes wide with horror. Had Chuck or Vera decided that she shouldn't be taking lessons?

"I see that you're as surprised as I was." Rachael absently tapped her pencil against the palm of her hand. "Do you know Joanne Tripper?"

Libby nodded, unable to speak around the rising anger.

"Her mother called Thursday and said that you'd be quitting soon and that Joanne could start immediately. I told her that you weren't leaving, but she seemed positive." Rachael's eyes narrowed thoughtfully. "That woman seems obsessed with the idea of her daughter's taking lessons from me. I hope they aren't putting pressure on you, Elizabeth."

"I can handle it. I can take care of Joanne!" Libby gripped her hands tightly in her lap. How she could take care of her!

48

"Don't be too hard on the girl. Remember she has a dream, too. She wants to be a concert pianist just as badly as you. And her mother is pushing her very hard, maybe too hard."

"I'm so glad that I'm taking lessons from you, Rachael." Libby remembered the day last summer when Chuck and Vera had brought her to play for Rachael. She had been very, very nervous, but Rachael had taken her as a student. Even though she was an aid kid with a lot of problems, Rachael had taken her. Nothing and nobody would stop her!

"Play this piece," said Rachael, tapping the page she meant. "Notice the timing."

Libby forced her anger away. Her hands stopped trembling as she found the right notes. She wouldn't think about Joanne now. She would concentrate on what she had to play.

"Play it again, Elizabeth. Think of what you're doing."

Libby flushed and played it again.

"That's much better. I want you to take this and this." Rachael picked up Libby's second book and found two more pages for her to practice. "Work hard on your piece for the recital. It's two weeks away and I want you to play your best."

Chills of excitement ran up and down Libby's back as she thought of playing in front of an audience. She would be the best pianist at the recital! Grandma and Grandpa Johnson were planning to visit and stay a few days so they could attend the recital.

"I remember my first recital." Rachael stood up and walked toward the group of pictures of herself in concert, then turned with a smile. "I was as excited as you, Elizabeth. My parents bought me a new dress and shoes. They had to save for weeks to buy them, but they wanted me to look my best while I played my best." She clasped her hands in front of her, a dreamy look on her attractive face. "Oh, I loved being in front of that audience and pleasing them with my music! After that, I worked harder than ever. I wanted others to be swallowed up with my music, to flow with it, to know every feeling I felt."

Libby stood beside the piano and watched Rachael's expressive eyes. "Will you ever do another concert?"

"I think about it. Of course I do. It was my life for several years. I might play a few local concerts." She shook her head with a slow smile. "Maybe I'll never get it out of my system. But I've chosen my life, Elizabeth. I want to be a wife and mother full-time. I wouldn't trade my baby boy for anything. No amount of applause or music or anything can take his place. I couldn't do both. Others do it all the time, but I don't have the energy." She walked toward Libby. "So, I'm training others to take my place. I exchanged my dream for a different dream."

"I never will!" Libby pressed her folded arms tightly against her thin chest. "I don't want to get married ever! I want to be a concert pianist for all of my life."

"Hold to that dream, Elizabeth. Never let it go until a bigger dream fills you."

"There is no bigger dream." Libby lifted her chin defiantly.

Rachael laughed a gentle, soft laugh. "Once I thought that, but I was wrong. I'm happy with my life now. If a bigger dream comes to you, Elizabeth, be happy with it."

"Never!"

"Wait and see." Rachael patted Libby's arm. "If you ever do get married, you might be able to have a music career along with a good marriage. Others do it all the time, but I couldn't. You don't need to worry about it now. You're only twelve years old. You have a long time to get ready for the future."

"Piano is my future." Libby didn't like to hear Rachael say that maybe a bigger dream would come along. It scared her a little. What if that happened? It couldn't! She wouldn't let it!

Rachael piled Libby's books together and handed them to her. "I think your mother is waiting for you already. See you next week. You tell Joanne if she's determined to have a career in music to find another teacher and get on with it. Tell her to stop wasting time fighting over a teacher. She doesn't need me to be a success."

"I would hate it if Joanne were taking from you and I couldn't. I'm glad you're my teacher." Libby smiled self-consciously. It was hard for her to tell how she felt.

Rachael laughed and shook her head. "Oh, but you're good for my ego!"

Libby felt warm and loved as she pulled on her jacket. She stopped at the door. "No matter what Joanne's mother tells you, I'm not going to quit piano with you."

"I'll remember that. See you next week."

Libby hurried down the sidewalk to the car at the

curb. She slipped into the seat and smelled the bananas in a grocery bag behind her. "Hi, Mom. Were you waiting long?"

Vera shook her blonde head as she started the car. "I was a little late. It took me longer in the grocery store than I thought it would. I couldn't believe that line at the check-out counter." She looked back, then pulled into the street. "If you're hungry, you can have an apple or a banana."

"Thanks." Libby reached back and broke off a banana. She remembered all the years that she'd gone without fruit because it was too expensive to buy. The Johnsons always had plenty of fruit. Vera said it was good for them. "Want a banana, Mom?"

"I think I would like one. They smell delicious."

Libby broke off another and pulled back the yellow skin and handed it to Vera. Libby liked bananas best when the skin was covered with little brown spots.

"How did the lesson go, Libby?" Vera laughed. "Do you realize that I still can't remember to call you Elizabeth even after I determined that I would?"

"It's okay, Mom." Libby dropped the skin into the plastic trash bag. "The lesson was great. I played very well today. Rachael thinks I'm going to be ready for the recital."

"I'm sure you will be. That's going to be quite a day for all of us. We'll be very proud of you while you're sitting there playing for us." Vera clicked the blinker light and turned. A truck roared beside her, then turned onto the expressway.

"Mom."

"Yes." Vera looked at Libby, then back at the street.

"Would you ever make me stop lessons with Rachael?" Libby's heart raced.

"Why would you ask me that?"

"I was just wondering." She hoped Vera didn't notice that she was trembling.

"Honey, we wouldn't make you stop taking lessons from Rachael."

"No matter how bad I got?"

"Naughty, you mean?" Vera's brow raised questioningly.

"Yes."

Vera turned onto the paved country road. "Libby, the only reason I would make you stop lessons is if you quit practicing or if you learned that you hated piano. We both know that won't happen. We would never punish you by making you quit piano." Vera smiled at her. "Does that answer your question?"

Libby leaned back in relief. "Yes."

Vera glanced at her watch. "My, it's later than I thought. Ben has a boy coming over to stay for the weekend."

"Who?"

"A new friend that he made at school. Ben said the boy needs friends and that he wants to show him a good time this weekend. Chuck said we'll take him for a ride in the wagon with Jack and Dan."

"I'll like that!" Libby laughed happily as she thought about the big gray team. At first she'd been afraid of them, but she'd learned that they were gentle and well-trained. "We can ride back and look at Ben's Christmas trees."

"That's a very good idea." Vera pulled into the long drive and Libby leaned foward to see the big, beautiful house that was her home forever now. She never got tired of looking at it.

"We're home," said Libby, smiling.

SEVEN
Ben's guest

Toby dashed to the car, a wide smile on his face. "Ben's friend is here already!"

"Good," said Vera as she reached into the back seat for a bag of groceries. "Here, Toby. This one is light enough for you to carry."

"I'm strong, Mom. I can carry two." Toby almost dropped the bag in his hands and Libby steadied it for him. "I guess I'd better come back for another one."

"Tell Susan and Kevin to come and help," said Vera as Toby walked toward the back door. She placed a heavy bag in Libby's arms and told her to set it on the kitchen table.

Libby carefully carried the bag into the house, wondering why Susan giggled and looked at her so funny as she walked past her. Libby could smell that Susan had just painted on fingernail polish. She made a face. How could Susan stand that stuff? Who wanted pink or red fingernails?

In the kitchen Libby carefully set the bag on the table next to the one Toby had carried in. She turned when Ben called her name. She smiled as Ben walked into the kitchen with his new friend. The smile froze in place. "What are you doing here, Jerry Grosbeck?" she asked sharply.

Ben frowned at her and she knew he thought she was being very rude. "This is my new friend, Elizabeth."

"What are you doing here, Libby?" asked Jerry in a strange voice.

"I live here."

"Is this the family who's going to adopt you?"

"I see you two know each other," said Ben, nodding. "I didn't think you'd have had a chance to yet since Jerry's new here."

"We've known each other for a long, long time," said Jerry sharply. "Libby used to beat me up."

"Jerry used to steal my food and I had to go to bed hungry." Libby could see herself in the small, lumpy bed crying herself to sleep night after night. It made her want to hurt Jerry right now for what he had done to her in the past. She locked her hands together behind her back.

"She stole from me!" Jerry glared at her. "Did you look for my medal? Do you have it?"

"What are you talking about?" asked Ben with a puzzled frown. He stepped aside as Susan and Toby walked in with more groceries.

"Some company, huh?" whispered Susan as she walked past Libby to put her groceries on the table.

Libby suddenly felt too hot for comfort. She pulled off her jacket and walked out of the kitchen with her

head high. Jerry could worry about the medal until
she was good and ready to tell him that she had
found it. Last night she'd opened her puzzle box that
her real dad had given her for her twelfth birthday
and she'd put the medal in the secret drawer. She had
planned to take it to school Monday for Jerry. Now,
maybe she'd keep it a while and tease him about it
until he hurt as much as she'd been hurt by him.

"Did you meet Ben's friend, Libby?" asked Vera as
she hung up her coat and pulled off her boots.

Libby nodded. She could smell Vera's perfume.
"He's in the kitchen with Ben. I already know him.
We lived in the same foster home when I was ten."

"What a coincidence! You'll have a lot to talk
about, won't you?"

"A whole lot," Libby said dryly as she rolled her
eyes.

"Don't you like the boy?" Vera laid her arm across
Libby's shoulders and walked slowly with her toward
the kitchen.

"He was mean to me, Mom. I don't like to have him
around to remind me of the past."

"We'll talk about it later," whispered Vera. She
dropped her arm and walked toward Ben and Jerry.

Libby wanted to run upstairs and stay out of sight,
but she knew she had to help put away the groceries.
She tried to ignore the conversation between Vera
and Jerry. She reached up to put a box of cereal into
the cupboard and Ben frowned at her.

"Don't be rude to Jerry again," he said in a very
low voice so that only Libby could hear. Ben was
dressed in blue jeans and a dark blue sweat shirt. His
red hair was combed neatly.

"Why didn't you warn me he'd be here?" whispered Libby. "I don't want him here!"

"He needs a friend. Don't cause any more trouble." Ben turned away and walked to Jerry. "Let's go outdoors and look at the horses, shall we? Do you like horses?"

Jerry shrugged. "Not much, but I'd like to see them."

Libby wanted to yell at him to stay away from Snowball, but she bit her tongue and kept quiet. Vera would scold her if she said that.

Jerry turned at the kitchen door. "Come with us, Libby."

"No!" She wanted to hide. How dare he ask her to go with them?

"Please come, Elizabeth," said Ben. "Susan will go with us too. We'll show Jerry all around."

"Let's go, Libby," said Susan, her blue eyes twinkling with mischief.

"Go ahead, honey," said Vera, patting her shoulder. "The little boys and I will take care of the rest of the groceries. You kids go out and have fun."

How could she have fun with Jerry around her? How could she survive with Jerry here at her own home? She wanted to forget about him, about her life before she came to live with the Johnsons.

"Come on, Elizabeth," said Ben with one of his special smiles for her. He knew she couldn't resist him when he was nice to her and smiled that way.

"All right! All right." She sighed as she walked with them to the back porch for her warm jacket and boots. Her blue jeans and gold sweater would help keep her warm. Oh, she didn't want to go with Jerry He'd probably make fun of Snowball.

"Will you hurry up, Libby?" asked Susan impatiently as she stood at the back door.

"I'm coming, Susan." Libby zipped up her jacket and followed Susan into the cold. Rex barked and ran to her. She rested her hand on his head and followed Jerry and Ben to the barn. Rex made her feel a little better. He seemed to like her better than anyone else. Goosy Poosy didn't. He liked Ben and Kevin the best.

The big white goose ran to Ben, honking loudly. Libby heard Jerry laugh and ask what in the world that thing was. Ben said Goosy Poosy was their pet goose and a very good watch dog.

"Libby, tell me why Jerry hates you so much," whispered Susan, barely able to keep from dancing with excitement. Her blue jacket matched her eyes. Red-gold hair peeked out from under the blue hood. He cheeks were pink from the cold.

"I don't want to talk about it!" Or think about it or be reminded of it, she thought.

"Don't get mad at me! I didn't do anything."

"You made me come out here and I didn't want to." Libby walked around a mud puddle and wished she could splash it on Susan just to make her mad.

"Jerry wanted you to come. I only wanted to find out why." Susan shrugged and wrinkled her small nose. "What do I care about your dumb life before you came to live with us? Maybe you should have stayed with some other family."

"Maybe I should have!" Tears stung Libby's eyes as she ran away from Susan into the barn after Ben and

Jerry. She had to be with Ben to hear him say something kind to her. He wouldn't like to have Susan be mean to her. She wouldn't think about the mean things she'd said to Susan.

Jerry walked toward her and she knew he wouldn't let her get away without talking this time.

"Libby, did you find my medal?"

She lifted her pointed chin. "Yes. And it's in my room and I'll get it for you when I'm good and ready."

"That had better be now!" He caught her arm and the grip hurt but she stood very still, her eyes boring into his. "I need it. Get it for me!"

"Elizabeth, get the medal for Jerry so he can enjoy his weekend with us." Ben stood in front of her with his feet apart, his hands on his hips. "Don't make him wait any longer. He told me that his dad is coming back and will want it."

Libby laughed mockingly. "His dad was supposed to come back a long time ago. Isn't that right, Jerry?" She saw his face turn red and the scar seemed even whiter. She had asked him once about the scar, but he'd gotten so angry that she'd never asked again.

"Dad will come for me!" Jerry dropped her arm and stepped back, just missing a barn cat's tail. "I know he will. I need that medal."

The door opened and Susan walked in. "Joe and Brenda have come to play a game of Monopoly. Let's go in, shall we?"

"Hi, Ben." Brenda walked to Ben with a wide smile on her pretty face. Her black hair hung down her back almost to her waist.

Joe looked at Libby with a grin. "Hi."

Libby's anger left and she smiled at Joe. She knew

he liked her and she liked him. She stood beside him while Ben introduced Jerry to them.

"Joe and Brenda live just up the road from us in that big white house with the pine trees out front," said Ben.

"Libby and Jerry once lived with the same foster parents," said Susan, and Libby wanted to stuff a pile of dirty hay in her mouth. Didn't Susan know when to shut up?

"How nice," said Brenda stiffly. She managed a smile at Libby, but she only stared at Jerry.

Libby knew she was thinking how dirty and ragged and unkempt Jerry looked. At least Ben would see that he took a shower tonight. Ben always kept very clean.

"Libby and I have to go in right now," said Jerry gruffly. "She's got something of mine she's going to give to me. Right, Libby?"

"I guess so." She walked to the house with Jerry, trying to think of something to say that would make him stop thinking so much about his medal. It wasn't that important. She heard the others laughing and talking behind her.

"Where is it?" asked Jerry impatiently as they hung up their jackets.

"In my room. I'll get it and bring it down to you."

"I'll go with you."

She frowned at him but he walked upstairs with her to her room. She heard his whistle of amazement at her red, dark pink, and pink room. She knew what he was thinking. At first, she hadn't believed that a room this beautiful could be hers.

She picked up the puzzle box and tried to open it

but he made her nervous the way he was standing over her, his face so intent that he looked crazy. "I can't open it. I'll have to find the directions."

"Hurry up!"

She opened the desk drawer and rummaged around in it, knocking out the letter from Mark McCall. Quickly she picked it up and stuffed it into her pocket. She didn't want Jerry to see it or read it.

"What's taking so long?" Jerry picked up the puzzle box and tried to open it.

"The directions are gone." Libby looked around with a puzzled frown. Where were the directions? "I'll find them and open this, but we have to go back to the others."

"I'll just smash this open."

She grabbed it from him and held it tightly against herself. "Don't you dare! My real dad gave that to me."

His shoulders drooped. "My real dad gave me the medal, Libby. I have to have it."

For one wild minute she wanted to hug him close. She felt his sadness and it made her want to cry. "If I don't find the directions, I know Chuck will open it when he gets home. You can have the medal then. Can you wait that long?"

He shook his head. "But if I have to, I will." He sighed as he walked to the door. "I need it bad, Libby."

"I'll get it for you. I promise." And she meant it. She wouldn't tease him about it again. She'd open the box and get the medal and give it to him, then he'd be happy. She smiled, but he couldn't as they walked downstairs together.

EIGHT
Grandma Feuder

Libby shivered as she knocked on Gramdma Feuder's door. Lapdog wriggled around Libby's legs, almost knocking her against the swing on the porch.

The door opened and warm air as well as the aroma of baking cookies rushed out. "Why, hello, Elizabeth. I'm sorry to say Adam isn't here. He went with his parents for the weekend to visit my boy Larkin."

"I came to see you, Grandma. I just had to get away from home."

Grandma stepped aside. "Come on in, honey. You look like you'd lost all your friends. Tell me what's troubling you." Grandma Feuder closed the door and commanded the two dogs around her feet to lie down where they belonged.

Libby walked toward the big round table where a mound of cookie dough sat on flour. Libby touched the chair where Teddy had always sat. Now he sat on her bed next to Pinky. "Do you still miss Teddy?"

Grandma's blue eyes twinkled as a smile creased

her wrinkled face. She patted Libby's arm with a work-worn hand. "I guess at times I do, but I'm pleased that he's with you. I had that teddy bear a long time and he made me happy. Now he makes you happy."

Libby wanted to bury her face in Grandma's warm neck and feel Grandma's arms around her, holding her until she felt like laughing and singing instead of crying. Grandma wasn't her real grandma, but everyone called her Grandma.

"Sit down, Elizabeth," said Grandma softly. "Sit down and I'll fix us a cup of hot cocoa. On such a cold, windy day hot cocoa will hit the spot."

Libby sat down and absently pushed a little pile of flour into the big pile. She was thankful that Vera had agreed to her coming to visit Grandma. Maybe Vera had realized just how hard it was to be in the same room with Jerry Grosbeck.

While the milk heated, Grandma pulled a sheet of cookies out of the hot oven. She lifted them off and placed them in neat rows on the counter beside the stove. "Take one, Elizabeth. They taste the best just out of the oven."

Libby carefully picked up a cookie. It was hot against her fingers and smelled warm and sweet. She hadn't eaten much lunch with Jerry Grosbeck at the same table, so she felt hungry.

A few minutes later Libby sat at the table with a mug of hot cocoa. She managed a smile as Grandma sat next to her. "It smells good." She pushed the melting marshmallow down and watched it bob back to the top.

"We'll drink our cocoa and then roll out another

batch of cookies. I want to take some to that new family that moved in on the other side of me."

"I didn't know anyone moved in. Do they have kids?"

"I saw two or three but they might have been visiting. Would you like to go with me when I take over the cookies?"

Libby hesitated. Should she? She leaned back in her chair with a sigh. "I guess not today, Grandma. I couldn't today."

Grandma nodded her white head. "Would you like to talk about what's bothering you?"

Libby suddenly felt too hot with her red sweat shirt on. "I don't know what it is. I guess maybe it's Jerry Grosbeck."

"Who's Jerry Grosbeck?"

Libby took a deep breath, then quickly told Grandma about Ben inviting Jerry over and her past experiences with Jerry. "Oh, Grandma! I don't know what's wrong with me! One time I want to punch him and hurt him, then another time I feel sorry for him and want to help him. I can't keep up with how I feel. And I can't be nice to him for very long at a time. I don't mean to be bad, but I am, and then my family gets mad at me." Libby locked and unlocked her long fingers. Lapdog whined and curled up at her feet, resting his head on her foot.

Grandma smiled and nodded thoughtfully. "It sounds like the old Elizabeth is having a war with the new Elizabeth."

Libby giggled. "Oh, Grandma."

"It's true, honey. When you were born again, you were given a new nature. But, unless you keep the old nature buried, you start acting like you did before you accepted Christ. You've been learning to live by what the Bible says, haven't you?"

Libby nodded.

"The Bible says that you are to be made into the image of Christ. In order to do that, you must reject—turn away from—all your actions, words, and thoughts that aren't Christ-like. If you say or do something that you know is wrong, then ask Jesus to forgive you, and go on from there." Grandma took Libby's hand in hers and held it firmly. "Honey, you must forget the past and go forward. You've turned your life over to God. The future is what counts as well as the present. Forgive the hurt that Jerry caused you in the past. Forgive it and forget it. Go on with your life."

Tears blurred Libby's hazel eyes and she brushed them away. "When I look at Jerry all the pain comes back. I feel like the same little girl again and it hurts so much!"

Grandma nodded. "I know. I know. But the good news about that is that Jesus will heal that hurt. Just ask him to, then thank him for doing it."

Libby fingered the handle of her cup. She watched the melted marshmallow spread across the chocolate. "Sometimes I think I want to stay mad at Jerry for all the bad things he did to me. I want to get even with him."

Grandma set aside her cup and reached for the rolling pin. Libby watched her push the dough down and roll it thin. Was Grandma mad at her for wanting to get even with Jerry?

"Elizabeth." Grandma looked up from rolling the dough. "You have to decide what is more important to you. Do you want to be like Jesus or do you want to get even with Jerry?"

Libby's face flushed red and she squirmed uneasily. She hadn't thought about it quite like that before. "I want to be like Jesus."

"If you mean it, then you must willingly forgive Jerry and love him."

Libby bit back a groan. She wasn't ready to forgive or love Jerry. Maybe she could just ignore him and pretend he wasn't around. How could she forget the many times she was whipped with a belt because of Jerry? How could she forget the times she'd gone to bed hungry because Jerry had taken her food? How could she forget how much Jerry had teased her and made fun of the way she looked?

"Would you like to cut out cookies?" asked Grandma with a wide smile.

Libby managed a smile. She was glad that Grandma didn't say any more about the problem. Grandma probably knew she wasn't ready to forgive Jerry and that she could *never* love him.

Libby reached for the round cookie cutter and carefully pressed it into the yellow dough. A piece broke off and she ate it. It tasted even better than the baked cookie.

"Press on the cutter a little harder, Elizabeth. You must cut all the way through or you can't pick up the cookie without tearing it apart." Grandma pressed on the cutter and lifted the cookie and carefully laid it on the cookie sheet. "My grandma taught me how to

make sugar cookies when I was about six years old.
Someday, you'll be teaching your children and
grandchildren."

"Oh, no!" Libby stepped back, her eyes wide. "I will
never get married! I am going to be a concert pianist
when I grow up. I won't let anything stop me!"

Grandma squeezed Libby's thin arm. "You hold on
to that dream, honey. You hold it tight. You can be a
concert pianist. You practice and you dream, but if

love for a man comes along, don't push it away. You can be a concert pianist if you're married just as well as if you're single. Don't be afraid to share yourself with another just because it might affect your dream."

"Did you have a dream, Grandma?" Libby brushed flour off her hands.

Grandma nodded with a smile "I had a dream of being a wife and mother. I wanted to be the best wife and mother in the whole world. And I worked at it with God's help and strength."

Libby didn't think that was much of a dream but she didn't say anything. She didn't want to hurt Grandma's feelings.

Grandma slid the cookie sheet into the hot oven. "Different folks have different dreams, Elizabeth. Your dream is bigger than most, but not any more important. My dream was just as important to me as your dream is to you."

"I bet Jerry Grosbeck doesn't even have a dream." Libby moved back so Grandma could wipe off the table. "All he can think about is his dad coming for him."

Grandma looked at Libby. "That's Jerry's dream, honey. He is living for the day his dad comes back for him. He's planning for that day and doing everything he can to make it happen. His dream is just as important to him as yours is to you."

"I didn't think about that. But what if his dad never comes for him? Jerry's been waiting for at least four years now."

"Jerry's world will crash around him if that dream doesn't come true—unless Jerry can find another dream. It's important to look at what we want, then decide on a plan of action. The world has no plan of action for Jerry. But Elizabeth, we know another way, don't we?" Grandma chuckled as she finished wiping off the table. "We know a spiritual answer for Jerry."

Libby leaned against the chair as she remembered how they'd prayed for Grandma's grandson to come home to her—and he *had* come home. "You mean we could pray for Jerry's dad to come home, don't you?"

Grandma nodded. "I sure do. And you and I know that God answers prayer! Why don't you ask Chuck and Vera to tell Jerry that God can help him, then all of you agree together in prayer for his dad to come back? Adam and I will agree with you right here at home."

Libby walked around the crowded kitchen, her hands locked behind her back. Would Jerry laugh at Chuck if he told him about God? Had Ben already shared Jesus with Jerry?

"Elizabeth, Jesus wants to meet Jerry's needs. Right now, Jerry needs his dad in a bad way. We have the help that Jerry needs. We can share it, can't we?"

Libby hesitated, then nodded. Maybe she'd even talk to Jerry herself. Maybe she'd tell him that the medal wouldn't bring his dad back, but prayer could.

But how could she talk to him if she couldn't forgive him?

NINE
Jerry's medal

Lapdog stopped at the driveway and barked sharply as Libby turned onto the road and walked slowly toward the Johnson farm. Cold wind blew against her and she huddled down inside her jacket. The fur around the hood felt soft against her face.

Was Jerry impatiently waiting for her to get home again so she could open the puzzle box and get out his medal? Chuck would be home soon and he would open the box. Libby frowned. Where had the directions gone? She had always kept the sheet in her desk drawer in case she forgot how to open the box. Maybe it had gotten pushed to the back of the drawer. She'd look as soon as she reached her room.

But did she really want to give Jerry his medal? Could she do what Grandma Feuder had said and forgive and forget?

A car whizzed past just as she reached the long driveway leading to the large house. Tall oaks and maples in the front yard were already naked for winter. A rope swing hung from an oak near the house. She liked to sit in it and swing and think and dream about her future.

Libby looked up at the house and wondered if Jerry was watching her from the living room window or even from Ben's room upstairs. Jerry wanted his medal as much as she wanted to be adopted by the Johnsons. She never should have taken his medal. She wrinkled her nose. At the time she had, she'd wanted to do the meanest thing she could think of.

Slowly Libby walked up the driveway, her hands deep in her jacket pockets, her shoulders hunched. Could she forgive Jerry? Could she forget all the terrible things from the past?

"Heavenly Father, I don't want to do anything that would keep me from being close to you," she said softly. "I want to be good and nice and full of your love. But I can't love Jerry Grosbeck! Will you help me?" Tears stung Libby's eyes and she blinked them away. Rex barked happily and ran to meet her, his long tail waving excitedly. Libby rested her hand on his head. "Rex, I'm glad you're my friend. I'm glad you don't get mad at me like the others do."

Libby stopped at the side of the house and lifted her face to the gray sky. "Heavenly Father, thank you for your help. I am glad that you love me. I love you."

Goosy Poosy honked from the chicken pen where Kevin had put him. Goosy Poosy didn't like being shut up with the chickens, but Libby was glad he wasn't free to run to her right now. It was hard to stand still and let the big white goose run up to her to be petted.

"I'm going in now, Rex. I hope Jerry doesn't do

anything mean to me. I hope I can find the directions to open the puzzle box." Libby stopped, her eyes wide. Why hadn't she thought to pray about that? When would she learn to let the Lord help her when she had a problem? Chuck said it was very important to put the Lord first always. She worried first, then thought about praying.

She stopped just outside the back door. "Heavenly Father, show me where the directions are to opening the puzzle box. Thank you. In Jesus' name." She smiled, then playfully flipped the rope hooked to the bell beside the back door. She would find the directions, open the box, and give Jerry his medal.

"And I will forgive him!" She smiled and the smile seemed to start deep inside her heart. She knew the Lord was helping her forgive. After forgiveness she knew God's love would follow. "Thank you, Father. I do forgive Jerry. You please forgive me for being wrong. I sure am sorry."

Libby managed to reach her room without anyone noticing her. She hurried right to her desk. She would find the directions. She hadn't looked carefully enough before. She looked thoughtfully at her desk, then frowned. What was different? She gasped, her hand at her mouth. The shiny puzzle box was gone!

"Jerry took it! I know he did. If he breaks it, he'll be very, very sorry!" She ran to her door and into the hall. Were the boys upstairs? She rushed down the quiet hall, then stopped outside Kevin's room. She'd heard a noise in his room. She'd check with Kevin, then she'd see Ben and Jerry.

Libby knocked. Something bumped, then the door opened. Kevin stood in the doorway, his face pale and his eyes wide. He looked very guilty to Libby and she wondered what he'd been doing.

"If you're missing homework again, don't look at me!" said Kevin sharply. "I didn't touch your homework."

"I didn't say you did. I want to know where Ben and Jerry are."

Kevin shrugged and started to close the door but Libby stuck her foot in it, then pushed it wide.

"What are you hiding, Kevin?" She looked around his room, then walked in. The direction sheet to her puzzle box lay on his carpet next to two comic books.

"I can explain!" cried Kevin, clumsily picking up the sheet of paper. "Don't get mad. I wanted to learn to open the puzzle box without looking. I didn't hurt anything."

Libby glared at him, her hands on her hips. "Did you walk into my bedroom without permission and take that? And did you take my puzzle box, too? I'm telling Dad on you!"

"Don't, Libby. Please, don't! I'll put them back and I'll never touch them again unless you say I can. I didn't hurt anything." Kevin pushed back his soft blond hair. His eyes were large behind his glasses. "I'll get your box right now. I didn't open it. Honest."

Libby knotted her fists. She would not hit Kevin! She would wait for him to get her box, then she'd walk away and forget what he'd done. She grabbed the box from him. "I'm telling Dad."

Kevin's face flushed red, then grew pale again. "Remember I didn't tell on you the last time you forgot to feed the sheep. I did it for you."

Libby pressed the paper and the box against her

thin body. Kevin had not said anything that time to get her in trouble. She hesitated and she saw his face brighten. "All right, Kevin. I won't tell. Tell me where I can find Jerry and I'll take the medal to him as soon as I open the box."

"They're in Ben's room working on car models."

Libby walked to her room and closed the door. Her hands were shaking as she sank down on the large round red hassock. Soon Jerry would have his medal and the war between them would be ended. And the war between the old Elizabeth and the new one would be over, too.

She spread the direction sheet out and carefully moved the hidden blocks the way it showed. Finally the box opened and the hidden drawer popped out. She lifted out the bronze medal and studied it closely. The words on it were worn down and she couldn't read them. How many hours had Jerry sat and rubbed this and wished on it that his dad would come back to him? Did he think it was like Aladdin's lamp?

Libby set the closed puzzle box on her desk with the direction sheet under it. Slowly she walked to the door. Her stomach tightened and a shiver ran down her spine. What would Jerry do when she handed him this medal? She looked at it in her hand, then opened the door and walked to Ben's room. Taking a deep breath, she knocked before she could turn and run.

"Go away, Kevin," said Ben from behind the door. "Play with Toby."

"It's me, Ben," said Libby in a squeaky voice. "I need to see Jerry."

The door burst open and Jery stood there in his ragged clothes. He smelled like paint and glue. A smear of red paint covered the lower part of the scar on his face.

"Here, Jerry," she whispered, her hand out, palm up. The medal felt heavy. She watched Jerry's face turn as white as the paper in Ben's hand. Finally he lifted the medal off her hand and held it, staring down at it as if he couldn't believe his eyes.

"I finally have it back. I can't believe it. I sure thought it was gone forever. Now Dad will come back to me. I know he will. He's got to!"

Libby turned to leave but Ben caught her arm. "Thanks," he said softly. "I'm glad you gave it to him."

Libby shrugged, but the words made her happy.

"Thanks, Libby," said Jerry as he blinked his eyes fast. He couldn't be crying, could he? Libby couldn't imagine Jerry Grosbeck crying.

"That's okay, Jerry." She turned to go.

"Libby, I'm sorry for stealing your food from you."

She stopped, then slowly turned. "Oh." She didn't think Jerry knew the word "sorry."

"I'm sorry that Mrs. Adair beat you all the time."

Libby bit the inside of her bottom lip to keep it from trembling. If she wasn't careful, she'd be crying in front of Jerry and Ben. "I forgive you, Jerry."

He blinked in surprise. "You do?"

She nodded. She wanted to tell him that she'd already forgiven him with God's help, but the words wouldn't come. Once again she turned to go.

"Libby."

She turned back, her eyes on Jerry questioningly.

"I'm glad that you have this family to adopt you." He self-consciously twisted his toe on the carpet. "If my dad wasn't coming for me, I'd want to be in this family, too."

"I'd like that," said Ben with a wide smile. "We could build models together all the time."

"I hope your dad does come back for you, Jerry," said Libby. She quickly turned away before he could see her tears. She didn't believe Jerry's dad would ever come back for him.Then she remembered that God answered prayer. They would pray for Jerry's dad to come get him. Someday she'd tell Jerry that they could pray and God would answer, but not today. He might not want to listen to her. It would be better to let Chuck talk to him about God and praying. Chuck would do a better job.

Libby walked into her room and closed the door. For a minute she just stood there, then she twirled around, laughing quietly with joy.

TEN
Sunday

Libby carefully hung her blue corduroy skirt in the closet next to the flowered blouse she'd worn to church. Her stomach tightened with hunger as she thought of the roast that she'd smelled downstairs. She loved the tiny carrots that Vera cooked with the meat.

Libby closed the closet door and tugged her sweater over her jeans. She picked up a comb to run through her short brown hair, then turned at a knock on the door. She frowned, hoping it wasn't Jerry. She didn't want to talk to him yet.

"It's me, Libby," said Susan, and Libby called for her to come in.

Libby smiled as Susan bounced into the room. Susan looked very pretty dressed in blue jeans and a long sleeved pink pullover blouse. Her long red-gold hair was hooked in a pony tail over each ear.

"Do you think Jerry liked Sunday school and church, Libby?" Susan could barely stand still in her excitement. "He sure was listening to Connie, wasn't he?"

Libby nodded. "I'm glad Ben let him wear his good pants and shirt. I know Jerry would've been very embarrassed if he'd gone dressed in his ragged clothes." Libby remembered the first time she'd dressed in church clothes and gone to Sunday school with the Johnsons. She had thought for sure that no one would know that she was an aid kid, but Brenda Wilkens had called her aid kid in front of everyone and embarrassed her. Libby flushed as she remembered how she'd pinched Brenda and made her squeal. Everyone had looked at them and Libby had wanted to sink out of sight under the pews. Now she knew most of the people in the church and liked them. They didn't seem to mind that she didn't really belong to the Johnson family. She had noticed that several people had talked to Jerry and he hadn't been rude at all. Maybe he liked them, even though he had said that he wouldn't.

"I heard Jerry tell Ben that he would come to church with us every Sunday if we'd pick him up. Dad says we can." Susan's blue eyes sparkled and her cheeks were flushed pink.

Libby's eyes widened and she gasped. "Susan, do you like Jerry for a boyfriend?"

Susan tipped her head back and laughed a soft, little breathless laugh.

"Susan!"

"He's nice, Libby. Maybe not always to you, but he is to me. I like him. I feel sorry for him."

Libby frowned and pushed her fingers into her

back pockets. "You're getting as bad about boys as Brenda Wilkens."

Susan wrinkled her small nose and shrugged. "I'm not like you, Libby. I can't bury myself at the piano every spare minute. I want to do something really exciting."

"You mean boys, don't you?" Libby wanted to shake Susan hard. How could Susan think boys were more interesting and exciting than playing concert piano? "I will never like boys! I won't go on dates or get married! I can't see how you can stand to think about boys!"

Susan doubled her fists at her sides and stuck her chin out. "Boys like me and I like them. As soon as Mom lets me, I'm going out with boys. And I might even go out with Jerry Grosbeck!"

Libby thought of all the bad words Jerry used and his terrible actions and she knew Vera wouldn't allow Susan to go with him. "Let's go eat dinner," Libby said impatiently. "I don't want to talk about boys now."

"Sure. You want to play your piano night and day and never take time for anything else."

Libby walked away from Susan. She would not argue any longer or she'd get mad and say something she'd have to apologize for later. She wanted the day to be enjoyable. She didn't want to have Susan angry at her while they took a wagon ride back to Ben's Christmas trees.

"I was beginning to think you girls didn't want to eat today," said Chuck with a smile as the girls sat at their places. The roast sat in front of Chuck with the knife and fork beside it. Libby's mouth watered at the sight and smell of the food.

Chuck thanked the Lord for the food, then picked up the sharp knife. "Who wants the biggest piece besides Toby and Kevin?" He grinned as he looked around the table. Libby watched Jerry's face and knew he was as surprised as she'd been to find a man as nice as Chuck Johnson. He could tease and laugh and he could be serious and kind. His red hair was combed neatly for once. He still wore his white shirt and tie that he'd worn to church. Libby knew that later he'd change into his jeans and sweat shirt before they went for the wagon ride.

Libby helped herself to a spoonful of yellow squash that Ben had raised in the garden. Everyone laughed and talked and helped themselves to food. Never in her life had Libby sat at a table like this one. Chuck and Vera wanted the kids to talk and enjoy the meal, not shovel down their food and leave fast. Libby peeked at Jerry. Was he enjoying it as much as she did? Often she had been sent to the kitchen to eat away from the family in other foster homes. She knew Jerry had also.

Slowly Libby chewed a piece of delicious meat. She was glad Vera was teaching her how to cook.

"I'll have to get my ad in the paper next week for my Christmas trees," said Ben as he buttered a roll.

"Some of my trees will be ready to sell this year," said Susan excitedly. "I'll use the money to buy clothes."

Vera shook her head. "Susan, Susan. You have enough clothes. Save the money for college, the way Ben is."

Susan frowned. "I'm not going to college. I'm sick of school."

Chuck laughed and wagged his finger at Susan. "You have a long time to go yet, so you'd better get unsick of school." He turned to Jerry. "Are you planning on college after high school?"

Libby knew what terible grades Jerry got in school. She saw his shoulders stiffen and she knew he didn't want to talk about school to this family who thought that everyone should attend college.

"I'm like Susan," said Jerry gruffly. "I'm sick of school."

Libby locked her fingers in her lap, afraid of what Jerry would say next. "I can't wait to ride in the wagon again," she said quickly. "I think Jack and Dan are anxious to take us."

Chuck pushed away from the table. "I'll go hitch them up while all of you get ready."

"And we'll have dessert when we get back," said Vera, standing up. "Libby and Susan made chocolate layer cake and we have vanilla ice cream."

"I want some now," said Kevin.

"You'd eat all of it if we let you," said Susan, playfully punching Kevin's plump shoulder.

"I lost two pounds last week," he said proudly. "Before long I'll be as skinny as Ben."

"Sure you will," said Ben, nodding. "You'll get that way by eating two helpings of dessert."

"I'll eat it for you just to help you out," said Jerry, with a grin.

Libby looked at him in surprise. She didn't think he would join in with the teasing and laughing. She saw his shoulders shake with his silent laughter. He really was having a good time with them. Maybe now he knew that all Christians weren't phony.

About an hour later Libby stood outdoors beside the big gray horses. She reached up and patted Jack's neck. She knew if he wanted to he could step on her and smash her into the ground but Chuck had said that Jack and Dan were very gentle, more gentle than the other horses.

"Climb in, Elizabeth," said Chuck as he stepped up to the wagon. "You can ride up front with me if you want."

A cold wind blew against her face as she climbed into the wagon and onto the seat with Chuck. Vera sat with Kevin and Toby. Susan sat behind them with Ben and Jerry. Libby looked down at the ground and smiled at Rex who stood ready to run along beside the wagon. Dan nickered and shook his harness. Libby knew he was anxious to be on the way. She remembered the first time she'd ridden in the wagon. She'd been afraid that she'd fall out.

With a creak and a lurch the wagon moved forward, the big grays stepping in perfect timing. Libby held tightly to the rough seat and pushed her feet against the wooden floor of the wagon. Was Jerry at all nervous? Had he ever ridden in a wagon pulled by horses?

Chuck stopped the team at a gate and asked Libby to open it for him. She jumped down, her legs a little weak. She fumbled with the gate, then pulled it open. She waited as the wagon rolled through. Jerry smiled at her and she almost fell over. Rex rubbed against her leg as she pulled the gate shut and hooked it securely. She ran back to the wagon and scrambled up.

Chuck slapped the backs of the horses with the reins and told them to get up. He smiled at Libby and she smiled back. "Elizabeth," he said in a voice low enough that only she could hear. "I talked with Jerry last night in the study. We prayed together for his dad to come home. Jerry doesn't know if praying will help, but he said if it worked for you, it might work for him."

Libby flushed and stared straight ahead at the horses' ears. "Jerry can't believe that I've changed. I guess he doesn't know that God does change people and that he can answer prayer."

"Jerry will learn. We'll help him all we can. He's a fine boy."

Libby looked at Chuck in surprise. Was he talking about the Jerry she knew? Didn't Chuck know what Jerry was really like?

"Jerry needs love, Elizabeth. He needs to know God's love and our love. I think you're the one who can help him the most. Share with him what the Lord has done for you."

Libby was quiet while the wagon rolled through the cattle pasture. A rabbit hopped out of sight in a clump of weeds. She didn't know if she could talk to Jerry about the Lord. She looked at Chuck. "I'll try, Dad. I don't know what to say though."

"Just tell him how you learned about God's love, then how God answered prayers for you."

"I'll try."

Chuck patted her knees. "You'll do it, honey. I know you will."

Libby thought about that as Chuck drove into the grove of Christmas trees. Last winter Libby had helped Ben bring the customers out to choose their own trees. She had liked doing it. Sometimes Ben would drive the wagon, but when there was enough snow, he'd drive the sleigh. She had had fun helping the Johnsons pick out a tall tree for their living room. They had even let her help decorate it. None of the other foster families had allowed her to.

Rex barked at a squirrel as Libby jumped from the wagon.

"Here are my trees, Jerry," said Ben proudly. "Dad and I planted these big ones when I was four years old."

"I never saw so many Christmas trees in all my life!" Jerry's dark eyes were wide as he slowly turned to look at all the trees. A large cardinal flew from a green branch and Jerry sighed and shook his head. "I never saw anything like this in my whole life."

Libby knew how he felt. She stood with her hand on Rex's head and looked around the quiet countryside. All of this belonged to the Johnson family. She was a part of the family, so that made this hers also. Could Jerry's life change as much as hers had? Would he have a family like this someday? Would he have a chance to belong to someone who loved him?

Tears stung Libby's eyes as she watched Jerry talk with the others. Silently she prayed for Jerry. With her whole heart she wanted him to find the happiness and love that she'd found. And she would talk to him about God. She would tell him all she could. Her heavenly Father would help her.

ELEVEN
Joanne's lie

Libby walked back into the English room and looked
around her desk. She'd left her book somewhere and
hadn't realized it until she'd finished eating lunch.
Her letter from Mark McCall had to be in the book.
She'd looked everywhere for it. The book wasn't on
her desk or on Mr. Wright's desk. Libby pressed her
lips together and narrowed her eyes in thought.
When had she last seen her letter from Mark? She'd
had it when she and Jerry had been in her bedroom
looking for his medal. She gasped. Jerry had probably
taken her letter to get even about the medal, then
not thought to give it back when she'd handed him
his medal.

She walked quickly into the hall and almost
collided with Jerry and Ralph Bauer.

"I want to talk to you, Jerry," she said sharply. She
looked away from Ralph quickly. She couldn't stand
to be near him.

"You can say anything in front of me," said Ralph

with a gruff laugh. "Me and Jerry are friends. He don't have secrets from me."

Libby wanted to grab Jerry away from Ralph, but she stood very still and looked at Jerry. She heard a giggle and looked up to find Joanne Tripper watching them with interest. Libby felt her face turn red and she stepped back into the English room. Much to her surprise, Jerry followed her, but Ralph walked away.

"What do you want?" asked Jerry impatiently. "Can't you ever leave me alone? You think because I stayed with the Johnsons this weekend that you can talk to me any way you want, anytime you want. I don't want you bothering me when I'm with Ralph. Got that?"

Libby stood with her fists on her hips, her head tilted sideways. "I got it all right! But do you have this? I don't want you to keep that letter of mine that you took when you were at my house. I want it back now!" Oh, she would like to pop him in the nose with her fist! How could he look so smug and sure of himself?

"I'll keep that dumb letter as long as I please." He turned to leave and she grabbed his arm.

"I want my letter now!"

"I won't give it to you!"

He stood just a little taller, but all her work on the farm made her much stronger. She jerked him hard and his head snapped. "I want my letter right now!"

He broke free and shoved her against the wall. "I knew you weren't different, Libby Dobbs! I knew you were the same ornery girl you always were."

Libby's hands dropped to her side and she wanted to cry. She didn't struggle when Jerry grabbed her

and shoved her into the small book room in back of
Mr. Wright's desk. When he slammed the door she
just stood there and stared at it. When the lock
clicked, she gasped and grabbed for the knob. It
wouldn't turn! "Jerry! Open this door right now!" She
waited, then called again. She rattled the knob, but
nothing happened. He had locked her in! Oh, that
mean brat! Just wait until she got her hands on him!
He'd be sorry for sure.

What was she thinking? She stepped away from
the door with her shoulders drooping. How could she
forget so soon? Why was she bad when she wanted to
be good? Silently she asked God to forgive her again,
then to help her do better next time Jerry did
something to make her mad.

Just then the door opened and Libby rushed out,

ready to tell Jerry that she knew he wouldn't leave her locked in.

"Into trouble again, Libby?"

Libby stared in surprise at Joanne Tripper. Naturally, Joanne had to be the one to free her. "I'm all right, Joanne. Thanks for getting me out."

Joanne flipped back her long blonde hair. "I thought Jerry Grosbeck was in there with you."

Libby opened her mouth to say that he'd locked her in, then closed it with a snap. Joanne would love to spread that story around.

"I told Mr. Wright that you and Grosbeck bought drugs from Bauer."

"You what?"

"I saw you both with him."

Libby's heart raced. How could Joanne do that? "We didn't buy anything from Ralph Bauer and you know it."

Joanne shrugged. "I know, but Mr. Wright doesn't. He'll believe me after all that trouble you've been in since he came."

Libby's thin chest rose and fell and she wanted to hurt Joanne, but she pushed the feeling down. "I won't get in trouble with Mr. Wright." She knew God was with her to help her in any situation. Silently she asked the Lord to stop the trouble that Joanne was trying to cause. She turned to the door at a sound. Mr. Wright stood with Jerry. Libby's heart sank.

"I understand that you're in trouble again, Libby," said Mr. Wright as he walked toward her in his usual strut. "I think you're working toward being expelled, aren't you?"

Libby swallowed hard and looked helplessly at Jerry. He looked down at the floor, his face red except the white scar.

"Joanne, you say you saw these two buying drugs?" Mr. Wright stood with his hands in his pants' pockets, his jacket open.

"I did!" Joanne stood with her shoulders back, her chin high.

"She did not," said Libby in a firm voice. "We were talking to Ralph Bauer, but we didn't buy anything. Jerry and I were talking about a letter of mine."

"We don't take drugs," said Jerry gruffly. "Libby's a Christian. She wouldn't do that."

Libby blinked in surprise.

"I saw!" cried Joanne, walking closer to Libby.

"I'll ask Ralph Bauer and let him tell you," said Jerry sharply. "You can search me and Libby if you want. We are clean. This girl only wants to get Libby in trouble because she wants to make Libby give up piano lessons so she can take from Libby's teacher."

Libby's legs felt weak and she sagged against Mr. Wright's desk. What was Jerry doing? Why was he helping her when he hated her? This had to be God's help for her. He was using Jerry to get her out of trouble.

Mr. Wright tapped a pencil against his palm while Joanne turned bright red, then pale. "I think we'd better drop the whole thing. Joanne, don't tell things that you can't prove, and Libby, stay out of trouble from now on. Jerry, Libby should be glad for a friend like you."

Libby felt an inch high. Friend! She had treated him terribly and he had still helped her. It couldn't be because they were friends. Maybe they weren't enemies, but they sure weren't friends!

"She was locked in your book room!" cried Joanne, pointing at Libby.

"Stop making trouble, Joanne," snapped Mr. Wright. "All of you get to your next class. The bell will ring any minute now."

Libby hurried out with Jerry close enough that she could feel him behind her.

"I didn't take your letter," said Jerry in a low, fierce voice. "I don't care if you believe me or not, but I didn't take it."

Before she could say more, he walked away into a crowd of students hurrying to class.

"I'll get you yet, aid kid!"

Libby stared at Joanne, speechless.

"I said I'd find a way to get you away from Rachael Avery. Momma says I have to take piano from her, and I'm going to." Joanne flipped back her hair and marched away.

"No, you're not!" whispered Libby between clenched teeth.

Just then April and May rushed up to her. "We just saw Jerry Grosbeck," said May breathlessly.

"He was leaning against his locker and he looked sick," said April. "Have you been fighting with him again?"

Libby frowned. "He just helped me out of trouble."

April laughed and nudged Libby. "No wonder he's sick. He probably shocked himself to death."

"He's probably trying to think of a way to kill himself for being nice to you," said May, laughing her tinkling little laugh.

"I'm going to see what's wrong with him," said Libby. She ignored the twins' surprise and hurried down the crowded hall. She found him standing at his locker, his forehead pressed tightly against it, his shoulders hunched. She touched his arm and he jumped.

"Leave me alone," he snapped in a low voice. "You always get me into trouble, don't you?"

"I do not! I didn't tell that you locked me in the book room!"

He frowned and shook his head. "I didn't lock you in. I pushed you in and shut the door because I know you don't like small, dark places, but I didn't lock the door."

She knew he was telling the truth. She licked her dry lips. "I believe you, Jerry. I bet Joanne did it to make sure we'd both get in worse trouble. But it didn't work." She stopped. "What's wrong with you, Jerry? Are you sick?"

He hesitated, then looked quickly around. He leaned his head close to hers. "I told Bauer I'd buy some stuff after school today. I needed to try something."

"Now you're sorry and you're afraid of what he'll do to you." Libby sighed. "Oh, Jerry. Don't do anything dumb. You know the Lord can help you, not drugs."

"I wanted to forget what Ben and his dad told me. I didn't want to believe them, but I know if they could take you and make you the way you are now, they must be all right. Mr. Johnson even prayed that Dad would come back to me, but I started thinking how impossible it would be for him to come for me, and I needed a way to forget it all. Ralph Bauer said that he could give me something that would cheer me up. I don't believe him now, but I did for a while."

"You just tell Ralph Bauer that you're not interested. And if you need help to keep him from beating you up, you call on Ben and me. We're strong!"

Jerry smiled hesitantly. "Thanks, Libby."

She looked down at her shoes. "That's all right. Thank you for helping me with Mr. Wright."

"That's all right."

She looked up and they both laughed. "I guess we'd better get to class," she said.

TWELVE
Trouble for Jerry

Joanne threw back her head and laughed and Libby wanted to shake her hard.

"What's so funny?" asked Libby impatiently.

"That Jerry Grosbeck won't think he's smart after Ralph Bauer gets done with him."

Libby's heart sank and a shiver ran down her spine. "What did you do, Joanne?"

Joanne stopped at the back of bus 8. The wind blew her hair across her face. She pushed it back and held it with her free hand. She carried books in her other hand. "I told Bauer that Jerry turned him in for pushing drugs. He said he'd get him."

"How could you do that?" Libby's hood fell back and cold wind blew against her and she shivered.

"It's too late for you to stop Bauer." Joanne ran to bus 8 and climbed in, her laughter floating behind her.

Libby stood very still, her heart racing. What could she do to help? Should she just go home and let Jerry take care of himself? She shook her head. She had to help him. But what could she do? Boys and girls pushed past her to climb on the buses. She had to do something fast. But what?

Silently she asked the Lord to help her help Jerry, to show her how to help him.

Just then April and May walked up to her.

"Quick, girls. We have to go help Jerry, but I have to get Ben and the others to go with us." Libby dashed into the bus and called Ben to come out and help her, then she begged the bus driver to wait a few minutes and she turned and ran back toward the school. She looked over her shoulder and almost stumbled. Ben, Susan, Joe, Brenda, Adam, Kevin, and Toby had all heard what Libby said and were following her, along with April and May. Jerry was getting plenty of help.

"Who are we helping?" asked Ben as he caught Libby's arm.

Quickly she told everyone what Joanne had said to her. Her head rang from the loud exclamations from the others.

"I know where Bauer does his business," said Joe, his dark eyes even darker with anger. "Follow me!" He ran around the school to the door outside the music room.

Libby bumped into Toby and almost knocked him down. She caught his arm and pulled him after her. Even Brenda was running, her long dark hair flowing out behind her.

"There they are!" shouted Kevin, pointing at two boys wrestling on the cold ground.

Libby caught Ralph's hair and tugged while Ben, Joe, and Adam hauled him away from Jerry. Jerry jumped up, holding his hand over his bloody nose. His jacket was ripped and his hair full of dirt and twigs.

"Listen, Ralph Bauer," said Libby, standing in front of him while the boys held him. "You see all of us? We're Jerry's friends. If you pick on him you have to answer to us. From now on, don't try to sell him drugs and don't beat on him. Understand?"

"You listen to Elizabeth," said Ben softly as he released Ralph. "We will help Jerry. He is our friend."

Ralph Bauer swore at them and ran around the school.

"Thanks," mumbled Jerry, his head down.

"Let's get to the bus before it leaves us," said Kevin.

"The bus!" cried Jerry. "I don't dare miss the bus! I'll be in trouble if I do." He raced around the school and the others followed. Libby thought they looked like a herd of horses all running fast in the same direction. She felt wonderful knowing that they'd helped Jerry. His nose had stopped bleeding but his jacket front and face were smeared with blood. What would his foster parents say?

"Catch the bus!" cried Adam, running alongside bus 12. He pounded on the door and the bus finally stopped and Jerry climbed on.

Libby watched April and May reach their bus just as the door was closing.

"Hurry, Libby," said Susan, pushing her toward the bus.

Libby stepped on and thanked the driver for waiting, then she walked back and sat down. Susan sank down beside her and looked at her with a wide smile.

"You sure did bring excitement into our lives, Libby. I never helped stop a fight before. I wish I could have pulled Ralph's hair for him like you did."

Libby sank down in her seat. She'd always wanted to be like Susan and stay out of trouble. How could a concert pianist go around fighting with others or even breaking up fights?

That made her think of Joanne. Libby was glad Joanne was riding a different bus or she knew someone would be breaking up another fight. How could Joanne be so mean? Did she really think she could get Libby to stop piano with Rachael Avery? Libby groaned. Tomorrow she would once again tell Joanne that she would never quit piano no matter how mean Joanne was to her. She had a feeling Joanne would be her enemy for life.

"What do you think Mr. and Mrs. McAlvey will do to Jerry?" asked Susan with a frown. "Will they kick him out for tearing his jacket and getting into a fight?"

"I don't know," said Libby barely above a whisper. She knew they might beat Jerry and send him to bed without supper. Or they might beat him and lock him in a closet like Mother had often done with her.

"You're scared of what they'll do, aren't you, Libby?" Susan's eyes were wide with concern for Jerry.

Libby nodded. She knew Susan had no idea what could happen. Susan had been born into the Johnson family. She didn't know how it was to be an aid kid who was taken in for reasons other than love. Of all the families that Libby had lived with, only the Johnsons had loved her. Susan didn't know about hatred and anger and fear.

Susan caught Libby's hand and squeezed it. Libby's eyes filled with tears and she blinked fast to keep them back. She couldn't cry in a bus full of kids who might laugh at her.

The bus stopped at Brenda and Joe's house but they said they were getting off at the Johnsons. Libby knew they wanted to talk about Jerry and what had happened.

With shaking legs Libby climbed off the bus along with the others. She smiled as Adam walked beside her. She knew he wanted to make sure she was all right. Wind blew against Libby and she shivered. She stood with the others talking about what had happened.

Finally Ben asked everyone to be quiet. "I think we should pray for Jerry. He might get into trouble with the people he lives with. Let's ask the Lord to protect and help him."

Libby smiled at Ben, glad that he'd suggested that they pray. She'd wanted to, but she couldn't find the courage. She should have known that everyone would agree to pray for Jerry. All of them knew the importance of prayer.

"Heavenly Father, we thank you that you love Jerry. Take care of him right now. Protect him and help his foster parents to be understanding and caring. Help Jerry to know that you love him. Thank you. In Jesus' name, amen." Ben looked around with a smile. "We agreed together on this and it will be answered."

Libby stood with them and talked, then Joe and Brenda said they had to go home. Adam left soon after. Libby watched him walk toward Grandma Feuder's home where he lived. She remembered how mean he was when he first moved in with his great-grandmother. Libby had felt sorry for him because he'd seemed so lonely. Soon they'd all become friends, then Adam had accepted Jesus as his personal Savior. After that his life had changed almost as much as Libby's had.

Susan poked Libby in the back. "I thought you didn't like boys. You're looking at Adam as if you're in love with him."

Libby's face flamed red and she glared at Susan. "I'm not like you, Susan."

"Race you to the house," called Ben, a few steps ahead of Libby and Susan.

Libby gripped her books tighter and ran as fast as she could up the long driveway. Rex ran out to meet her, barking happily. She reached the back door just two steps behind Ben.

"You almost did it, Elizabeth," he said with a wide grin. "I think I'm going to have to work out more so that you don't get faster than me." Ben's face was flushed almost as red as his hair and his hazel eyes sparkled with life.

"I'll work out more than you, then I will beat you." Libby laughed as she walked in and pulled off her jacket. She frowned at her English book as she thought of all the homework she had to do. It was getting harder and harder to find extra time to practice the piano.

"Hello, kids," said Vera from the doorway. "Did you

have a good day, all of you? Come in and tell me all about it while you eat your snack."

Libby hid a grin. What would Vera think after she heard about their adventure?

The smell of hot cocoa made Libby's mouth water as she walked into the kitchen. She loved Vera's hot cocoa and fresh rolls.

"Libby, I found something of yours when I did the washing today," said Vera, holding an envelope out to Libby.

Libby looked, then gasped. "My letter from Mark McCall! Where did you find it?" She took the letter and pressed it to her.

"In the pocket of your jeans."

Libby clapped her hands to her mouth as she remembered stuffing the letter into her pocket so that Jerry couldn't see it. And she'd accused him of taking it! Tomorrow first thing she'd tell him she was sorry. She would have to learn not to accuse anyone of anything again until she knew for sure that they were guilty.

"Here's your cocoa, Libby," said Vera as she set a mug of steaming cocoa on the kitchen table.

"Thanks, Mom." Libby sat down, her letter grasped tightly in her hand. Maybe she should call Jerry tonight to apologize. She nodded. She would. After chores, she'd call him and talk to him.

THIRTEEN
April and May

Libby looked out the basement window with an impatient frown. It was still raining. When would it snow? Ben needed snow for his Christmas tree business. Just two more weeks and he'd start having customers coming to cut down Christmas trees.

She turned from the window and smiled at April and May. They'd had permission to ride the bus home tonight with her and stay until eight.

"Let's play Ping-Pong," said Susan, picking up a paddle. "April, you be my partner and May can be Libby's."

Libby picked up a blue paddle and stood ready. She wasn't very good at Ping-Pong, but she was learning. Darts was the game she was very good at. She could even beat Chuck.

"Ready?" asked Susan, poised to volley for serve.

Libby missed the fourth time over and Susan got the serve. She danced around excitedly, then hit the ball. It didn't take long for Libby and May to lose. Libby grinned and May shrugged her shoulders.

"We can't win everything," said May with a laugh. "But it would be fun to win once in a while."

"I want to show you girls my new dress," said Susan, heading toward the stairs.

Libby started to follow, then stopped as a movement caught her attention out in the yard. She frowned as she watched. Someone was outside and just going into the horse barn and it wasn't anyone in this family. In fact the person looked a lot like Jerry Grosbeck. "I have to go outdoors for a minute and I'll be up later," said Libby, making sure she didn't sound too excited. She had to investigate alone. But maybe she was thinking too much about Jerry. She'd called him the other evening and told him she was sorry. He had barely talked and he hadn't been to school since. She had wondered why, but hadn't wanted to call him. Ben had called once but the McAlvey's had said he was busy and couldn't come to the phone.

Icy rain lashed against Libby as she ran across the yard to the barn. What if a stranger had gone into the barn? Why hadn't she thought of that soon enough to have Ben come with her?

"Libby, wait for me."

She turned impatiently to see April running toward her, her head down against the cold rain.

"I thought you were looking at Susan's dress."

April wrinkled her nose. "Who wants to see a dress? I knew you were up to something, so I followed you. What's up?"

Libby hesitated as she looked from April to the barn.

"Hurry, Libby! We're getting soaked!" April pushed her and they ran through the mud to the barn. April dropped her hood back and looked at Libby. "Now, tell me."

Libby fumbled with her hood, then turned on the light. Snowball nickered and Apache Girl neighed.

"You're stalling, Libby. What's going on?" April brushed her light brown hair away from her face. She looked ready to explode with curiosity.

Libby stood close to April. "I saw someone come in here. I think it's Jerry Grosbeck."

"Oh, my! And you think he ran away like May and I did?" She clutched Libby's arm. "If he ran away, it's for a good reason. Jerry always did take a lot from foster parents. Something terrible must have happened to make him run."

"I know."

A cat rubbed against Libby's leg and she picked him up for comfort. He purred loudly and she was glad he blotted out the wild beating of her heart.

Slowly Libby walked with April down the aisle. April pointed at the stacked bales of hay and Libby nodded. That was a sure place to hide. She had often hidden there while they all played hide and seek.

"Jerry," called Libby. "Come out. I know you're in here. I want to help you."

Dan snorted and stamped his big hoof. Snowball nickered again and stuck her nose over the stall door.

"Jerry, it's me, Libby. I want to help you. April's here with me. We know you came to us for help. We won't make you go back until we help you." She waited, the cat tightly against her. "Please, Jerry."

Slowly he walked out of an empty stall and stood in the concrete aisle. His face was bruised and one eye swollen shut.

"Oh, Jerry," whispered April, her hand at her mouth. "Oh, my."

"Jerry, Jerry." Libby walked toward him, a bitter taste in her mouth. "Who did this to you?"

Tears filled his eyes and ran down his bruised face. The scar stood out vividly. "I . . . I found my dad. I learned where he was and I went to see him. I had to hitchhike for half a day to get there. He . . . he didn't want me. He yelled at me and swore at me and he did this when I wouldn't leave." Jerry slumped down on a bale of hay and covered his face with his hands. His shoulders shook and loud sobs escaped him.

Libby sat on one side of him and April the other. Tears rolled down Libby's face and she saw tears on April's face, too. Jerry's dream was shattered. What would he do now for a new dream? How could he live, knowing that his dad didn't want him?

He would have to live with it, Libby knew. She had learned years ago that Mother didn't want her. One day she realized she didn't want Mother. God had given her a wonderful family and he did the same for April and May. He could do the same for Jerry Grosbeck.

Finally Jerry lifted his head. "Now I remember how I got this scar. As soon as Dad hit me, I remembered. He was drunk one night and he broke his whiskey bottle and came after me with it. I tried to get away but I was little and couldn't run fast. He caught me and did this." Jerry rubbed his finger down the white scar. "He wanted to kill me today, but I got away."

April knuckled her tears away. "Oh, Jerry. I'm sorry."

Libby swallowed hard and wiped her tears. "You can find a family to love now, Jerry. All this time you were saving up your love for your dad, now you can give that love to others around you."

He wiped his sleeve across his nose. "I'm going to stay here, Libby. This is the only family with any love. I'm going to stay here if I have to live in the barn the rest of my life."

Libby took a deep breath. "Let's go in the house and you can talk to Ben."

Jerry jumped up, his eyes flashing. "He can't make me leave!"

"He won't, Jerry. Ben cares about you. He'll find some clean clothes for you and Mom will fix you something to eat. When Dad comes home, he'll know what to do."

"You could hide me out here," said Jerry urgently. "You could keep me in here and bring me food and a warm blanket."

April shook her head. "May and I ran away from our foster home and came here. Libby hid us for a few days but she got in trouble for doing it. This family works together to help others. They won't send you back until they can be sure you'll be treated right."

"Let's go inside, Jerry." Libby tugged on his arm and he finally walked with her toward the door. What would happen if this time Chuck couldn't help. What would Jerry do if he had to go to a family who didn't care about him, who would beat him?

The rain had turned to sleet and Libby bent her head against it. It stung against the side of her face and she pulled her hood forward as she ran to the back porch. She pulled open the door and held it for April and Jerry. Thankfully she stepped inside and pulled off her wet jacket and boots. The warmth of the house enveloped her and she couldn't wait to lie in front of the fireplace in the family room.

"Mom."

Jerry caught Libby's arm and frowned. "Don't let her know I'm here. She might send me back to the McAlveys."

"She won't," said April with assurance. "She's great. She took care of me when I got sick. She loves kids a lot."

"She does," said Libby softly.

Vera poked her head out of the kitchen door where delicious smells of escalloped potatoes and meat loaf drifted out. "Did you call me, Libby? Oh, hello, Jerry. How nice to. . . ." She stopped and her eyes widened. "What happened to your face? Come in here this minute and let me take care of it."

Jerry held back but Libby urged him forward until he was walking with Vera to be cleaned up.

"I'll call Ben," said April. "Jerry will feel better if Ben is with him."

Libby nodded as she walked toward the family room. Cartoons were on TV and Kevin and Toby lay on the floor watching. Libby wanted to sit at the piano and play, but she didn't want to force the boys to turn off the television. Soon they'd have to shut it off, so she'd just wait. She sank down on the floor in

108

front of the fireplace. A log crackled and flames shot up the chimney. Sometimes it was hard to believe this was really her home.

By the time Chuck came home, Jerry was sitting contentedly in the family room playing checkers with Ben. Libby played her recital piece over and over. She would play it well by next week. She would make her family proud of her.

Chuck tapped Libby's head and she turned with a smile. "Hi, honey," he said as he bent to kiss her cheek. "I see you brought me someone else who needs help." His voice was too low for anyone else to hear him.

"His dad did that to him," she said in a low whisper. "He lost his dream."

"He came to the right place for help." Chuck walked across the room and greeted Jerry and Ben. "I'm glad you came, Jerry. Shall we go eat supper now and talk later?"

Libby watched the smile that spread across Jerry's face. She knew how it felt to be cared for, It would be great if Jerry could stay with them. At least in *this* foster home he wouldn't steal her food and she wouldn't have to beat him up.

"Coming to supper, Elizabeth?" Chuck held his hand out to her and she caught it and held on tightly.

FOURTEEN
Happiness is . . .

Libby sank dejectedly into her seat in English class. She had not had time to finish her homework. Chuck had called the McAlveys to let them know where Jerry was. They had agreed to let Chuck try to help Jerry. Then he had talked with Jerry a long time in the study, then with both of them. Jerry had finally agreed to go home to the McAlveys for a trial stay. He had confessed that he hadn't tried to love them and he hadn't allowed them to be close to him.

"I know Ed and Patsy McAlvey," Chuck had said. "They are kindhearted people, but they need to have you meet them halfway, Jerry. Will you try? If it doesn't work out, I'll help find you a loving home."

Jerry had agreed to try, much to Libby's surprise. He didn't seem upset that he had to go to them. Whatever Chuck had said before she came into the study must have changed his mind about going back to the foster home.

"Libby," said Joanne Tripper sharply. "Did you give up piano yet?"

Libby turned with a wide smile. "Joanne, I'm glad you asked. I will never give up piano with Rachael Avery. But you'll give up trying to make me quit. If you don't, my momma will talk to your momma and then we'll see who will stop making trouble." Libby laughed outright at the look on Joanne's face.

"Your mother is Marie Dobbs. She doesn't scare Momma."

"My mother is Vera Johnson. Does your momma want her calling on the phone to tell her to have you leave me alone?"

Joanne's face paled and she fumbled with the pencil she used to poke Libby. "So? Let her call. Who cares?"

"Your momma might." Libby turned around and folded her hands on her desk. She smiled. Just last night she'd talked to Vera about Joanne's threats.

Vera had told her what to do. That should take care of smart Joanne Tripper.

Libby felt a snap on her arm and she looked up to find Jerry shooting a paper wad at her. He smiled and stuffed the rubber band in is pocket. Libby stared at him in surprise. His hair was cut neatly. His shirt and jeans were new and fit him well. What had happened at the McAlvey's home last night? She managed a smile, hardly able to sit still. She wanted to ask Jerry right now what had happened. How could she sit through Mr. Wright's English class today? And what would he do to her for not having her homework completed?

Just then a tall woman walked into the classroom. Libby gasped. It was Miss Morrison! The classroom buzzed with surprise.

Miss Morrison stood behind her desk with a broad smile. "Good morning, class. I hope it's not too much of a disappointment to see me here. My mother is recovering nicely, so I came back a little early."

Libby sagged in her seat, her heart leaping with joy. The Lord had answered in a super fantastic way!

"I hear that Mr. Wright loaded you down with homework. I hope you won't mind going back to my policy of having no homework unless you can't finish something in school."

Libby cheered as loudly as everyone else. She wanted to run up and hug Miss Morrison. Now she'd have extra time to practice piano. Someday when she was a famous concert pianist she would tell the world that her English teacher had had a part by dropping homework. Libby smiled dreamily.

A cold sun shone through the windows but to Libby

it felt as bright and as warm as the summer sun. Nothing was going to ruin this day for her. She pulled out her notebook and wrote:

Happiness is . . .
seeing Jerry happy and well dressed.
having Miss Morrison back in English.
stopping Joanne's constant pestering.
being a concert pianist.
living with the Johnson family.
loving God and being loved by him.

Libby smiled as she read what she'd written. She would keep that page in her notebook and she'd add to it every time she thought of something. Her stomach growled and she grinned as she added a new line, "going home to eat Mom's cooking instead of school food."

She jumped when the bell rang. She could talk to Jerry and find out what had happened to him. She hurried to him but Susan beat her.

"You look great, Jerry," said Susan, almost bouncing up and down. "What happened? Did the McAlvey's put you in a different home? Who cut your hair? How did you get these new clothes so fast?"

Libby squeezed Susan's arm. "Give Jerry a chance to talk, will you?"

"Sorry, Jerry." Susan walked beside him into the hall and they stopped just outside the door.

"Jerry!" cried April and May together. "Is it really you?"

Libby saw him flush, but he smiled at them and said it really was. Libby wanted to ask him a dozen questions too, but she knew the twins and Susan had already asked him more than he could answer.

"Let's go to lunch and talk there," said Susan, motioning toward the lunchroom.

Libby filled her tray with the usual Friday menu. She didn't like chili very much but it wasn't bad with a lot of crackers crumbled up in it. She sat down and impatiently waited for the others to sit down and be quiet so Jerry could talk.

Jerry drank his apple juice and wiped his mouth with the back of his hand. "Mr. Johnson talked with the McAlveys and me last night. He told them about my dad and what had happened. They felt real bad about it. I guess I didn't think they'd care. They want me to call them Mom and Dad." Jerry flushed self-consciously. "I said I'd try to. But it's hard to get used to it after saying all along that I didn't want anything to do with them. I wanted Dad, and nobody else would do. Now that I'm getting to know . . . Mom and Dad . . . I like them a lot. And they like me." He rubbed his hand across his chest. "They had bought all these new clothes for me but I said I hated them and wouldn't wear them. I said I'd wear my rags before I'd take anything from them." Jerry looked at Libby and smiled at her. Her heart skipped a beat and she smiled back. "Libby, I know that God did change you. Last night I prayed and asked Jesus to change me. I'm a Christian now, too. And I won't be that old rotten Jerry again."

Libby couldn't speak around the lump in her throat but the others made up for her silence. God had answered for Jerry better than they'd even imagined. Libby smiled. Could this happy boy really be "gross

Jerry Grosbeck" whom she'd hated for so long? Right now she felt like hugging him. She would not dare do that or Susan would think he was her boyfriend.

Finally Jerry finished talking and eating. He stood up. "I'm going to find Ben so I can tell him my good news." He carried his tray and walked away.

"That is the happiest story I've ever heard," said Susan with a sigh, her eyes on Jerry until he walked out of sight. "That's better than a TV program."

"I think I'm going to cry," said May, wiping at her eyes.

"Let's get out of here before she does," said April, standing up quickly. "May cries loud."

Libby walked with the girls out of the lunchroom. She stopped as Joanne walked up to her.

Joanne stood with her hands at her narrow waist. "You'd better find that friend of yours. He's buying stuff from Ralph Bauer again."

"Do you mean Jerry Grosbeck?" asked Libby.

Joanne nodded.

"Never," said April, as May burst into laughter. "Never, never, never."

"I don't know why you want us to find Jerry right now, Joanne, but we will never believe that lie about him again. Jerry would not buy drugs at all. He's a Christian just like we are. You'll have to stop lying about him, Joanne. It won't work."

Joanne turned with a loud sniff. "You're all a bunch of dumb Christians. Just stay away from me from now on."

Libby smiled. She'd stay away from Joanne until she found a chance to tell her about the Lord. When the Holy Spirit told her to talk to Joanne, then she would. In the meantime she'd pray for Joanne. Just look what miracles had happened already!

Libby walked down the hall and stopped to look out the big glass doors. "Girls, look! It's snowing!" Libby pulled out her notebook and added at the bottom of her "happiness is" list, "the first snow of winter."

If you've enjoyed the **Elizabeth Gail** series,
double your fun with these delightful heroines!

Anika Scott
Fascinating stories about an
American girl growing up in Africa.

#1 The Impossible Lisa Barnes

#2 Tianna the Terrible

#3 Anika's Mountain

#4 Ambush at Amboseli

#5 Sabrina the Schemer

Cassie Perkins
Bright, ambitious Cassie discovers God
through the challenges of growing up.

#1 No More Broken Promises

#2 A Forever Friend

#3 A Basket of Roses

#4 A Dream to Cherish

#5 The Much-Adored Sandy Shore

#6 Love Burning Bright

#7 Star Light, Star Bright

#8 The Chance of a Lifetime

#9 The Glory of Love

You can find Tyndale books at fine bookstores everywhere.
If you are unable to find these titles at your local bookstore,
you may write for order information to:

Tyndale House Publishers
Tyndale Family Products Dept.
Box 448
Wheaton, IL 60189